Frederick R Sanford

The bursting of a boom

Frederick R Sanford

The bursting of a boom

ISBN/EAN: 9783743329706

Manufactured in Europe, USA, Canada, Australia, Japa

Cover: Foto ©Andreas Hilbeck / pixelio.de

Manufactured and distributed by brebook publishing software
(www.brebook.com)

Frederick R Sanford

The bursting of a boom

THE

BURSTING OF A BOOM

BY
FREDERICK R. SANFORD.

––––––––

PHILADELPHIA:
J. B. LIPPINCOTT COMPANY.
1889.

THE BURSTING OF A BOOM.

CHAPTER I.

It all came about by accident, while Warren has always insisted that the fault, if fault there were, was to be charged upon the weather. It was a most deplorable morning on which to make a journey, raining as it can rain only in Southern California on those rare occasions when, in the land of sunshine and flowers, a storm does occur; then, in very truth, the rains descend and the floods come. On an average of three hundred and fifty days in the year Los Angeles is a beautiful city: on the fifteen remaining days, when it may be safely counted upon to rain, few will be attracted by its charms; while certainly its least attractive part is the vicinity of the Southern Pacific depot.

As Warren sprang out of the carriage upon the depot platform and looked around upon the street, no longer a street, but now resolved into an indescribable chemical compound of earth held in solution by water, he said to himself, "In California, most assuredly, it never rains but it pours: it is a certainty that the originator of that wise proverb was a native of the Golden State."

3

Hurrying through the dripping mass of humanity with which the platform was thronged; dodging here an umbrella, there deploying to make his way safely around a lady who, with true feminine unconsciousness of all the possible damage which she might inflict upon the temper and the raiment of her fellow-mortals, was vigorously shaking the water from her rubber cloak preparatory to folding it, wearing all the time that sweet air of unconscious innocence of wrong intention which so completely disarms the irate males in her vicinity, reducing them to silent helplessness; dexterously avoiding this extemporized shower, Warren made his way to the baggage-room. Time was pressing, moments were precious, for he had been late in leaving his hotel; but for once fortune favored him: no one else was in the room, and right by the door was his trunk with his initials—M. H. W., N. Y.—stencilled upon each end.

"Here, captain, check this to Ventura!" he called out to the baggage-master.

"Ventura it is," that functionary responded, detaching from its strap as he spoke the brass tag with its paper card, denoting the destination of the baggage, which California roads employ. As Warren passed out of the door he brushed past a young lady swathed so completely in india-rubber that no part of her face was visible; and as he slowly made his way down the platform, looking back at her, and wondering, after the manner of young men, whether she was pretty or plain, light or dark, he narrowly escaped being run down by the heavily-loaded truck bearing his trunk among many others to the train.

Entering the smoker, Warren threw off his water-proof, folded it, placed it in the rack, removed his overcoat, drew on a skull-cap, and with a cigar and a novel proceeded to while away the seventy-odd miles of distance and four hours of time lying between Los Angeles and San Buenaventura.

I think it is Charles Lamb who says, "He who doth not smoke hath suffered no great disappointment, known no great sorrow, and hath lost the great con-solation in life." What man, young or old, does not endorse this sentiment and bless the memory of those noble red men who first among mankind discovered the manifold delights of tobacco? Surely its uses and its blessings must have been revealed to them in a moment of inspiration; because it was to them, the aborigines of a land whose vast territory could be annihilated, and its inhabitants brought into close sympathy with each other only by railroads, and were destined to be railroad travellers as an inevitable conse-quence: to the aborigines of such a land was revealed first among living men the delights of a weed which can turn even the long and otherwise weary transcon-tinental journey into a constant revelation of progres-sive bliss.

Without tobacco what man could endure the three thousand miles of physical discomfort involved in the transit over the continent? Without the solace of his cigar what man would possess sufficient hardihood to undertake those six weary days and miserable nights, or the agonies only known to him who, by bitter ex-perience, has learned how leisurely the speed and how wretched the coaches of the A. T. and S. F. R. R. Co.?

Not even all the delights awaiting them in California would entice the male portion of humanity across the continent in the face of these actual hardships did they not have this consoling weed to soften their sorrow and while away their weary hours. Yet it can be done! It is done every day—by the women! I do not know the secret of this phenomenon, unless it be owing to their superior patience and bravery; or unless it be that caramels are to them what tobacco is to their husbands and brothers,—a source of consolation and the well-spring of physical endurance and of mental and moral strength.

The ride from Los Angeles to San Buenaventura is beautiful, while the whole country traversed is also full of interest. Long reaches of fertile fields and rich valleys sweeping down from the mountains to the ocean call forth one's constant admiration. The train rushes through the San Fernando tunnel, then on past the Camulos ranch, overflowing with interest to all California tourists; for are not all California tourists Ramonolaters? And here Mrs. Jackson painted the scenery and gathered the legends and myths whose picturesque blending makes up the tale which calls forth so much enthusiastic devotion towards this now world-famous ranch.

But Warren was not a Ramonolater; therefore he did not gaze spellbound upon either the whitened adobe ranch-house embowered amid orange-trees, or the great wooden crosses which crown the hill overshadowing the track, "to tell all passers-by that good Catholics live here;" and the sole interest possessed by the Camulos in his eyes lay in the fact that it was in

Ventura County,—a fact which assured him that his journey was gradually coming to its end.

On sped the train into the beautiful Santa Clara Valley of the South, the garden-spot of Southern California. Now the short winter's day was drawing to its close; nothing could be seen as the cars whirled along save, now and then, a light, as the train shot by some lonely ranch-house; so, even had he desired other diversion, none remained for Warren save his book and his cigar. At last the lights grew thicker: the train was entering some large town; above the roar of the cars and the pelting of the rain-drops the moan of the ocean could be heard as the surf rolled in to break upon the beach. Slowly the train drew up before a brilliantly-lighted station, and Warren's California pilgrimage was at an end.

The brakeman thrust his head through the partially-open door, calling out, "San Buenaventura!" and at the discordant but welcome sound Warren slowly rose, gathered together his luggage, rearrayed himself in slouch hat and waterproof, and making his way through the throng of rival hotel-runners, each shouting the name of his hospitable hostelry at the top of lungs whose lusty strength proclaimed the wonders wrought by this genial climate, and interrupting a hackman in the middle of his chant, "Two bits to any part of the city," he asked, "Do you know Mrs. Elkins, of Poli Street?"

"You bet, captain," was the answer.

"Take me there," Warren demanded.

"All right, colonel! Checks?"

A ride at night through the streets of an unfamiliar

town always seems almost interminable; therefore a journey which seemed to Warren miles in length, but which was in reality but little more than half a mile, brought him to the house which was to be his home for many months to come.

It was a large white house lying well back from the street, with a well-kept lawn in front and around it; this lawn was filled with roses, now in full bloom: here and there were orange- and lemon-trees, their yellow fruit standing out in sharp contrast against the background of green leaves, and their blossoms filling the air with a delicious fragrance, while two giant fan-palms stood like exaggerated posts, one on either side of the entrance. All this Warren learned, of course, later on; no one, however profound his interest, would stop to pursue close and critical investigations into his surroundings in a dark night and under the drenching down-pour of a California winter rain.

His sensations had already informed him that the house stood on a street which ran up the side of a steep hill; while he could not fail to observe that it was a two-story edifice, and in this fact was an exception to the prevailing style of architecture in Southern California.

Warren, though in the unamiable frame of mind which is discernible even in the sweetest of dispositions at the end of a long journey made under uncomfortable circumstances, could not fail to be pleased with his quarters. The room was large, with a deep bay-window at the side opposite the bed, while two other windows, one on either side of the dressing-table, gave promise of abundance of light and air. The gas,

although it was turned low, still gave sufficient light
to enable him to see at a glance that the furniture was
of the kind most suitable to the country. The floor
was covered with matting; the chairs and the lounge
were of wicker seated with cane, making them perfectly
adapted to a country where, month after month, the
sun rises to set again in a cloudless sky, while even the
lightest of summer showers never moistens the ground,
and therefore the most careful and painstaking housekeeping cannot altogether vanquish that foe most hated
in a housewife's soul,—dust.

Having made his supper at Santa Paula the calls of
hunger did not compel Warren to defy the rain, therefore, having paid and dismissed the driver, he at once
began unpacking and setting in order his household
gods. Unlocking his trunk, he threw back the lid,.
then instantly started back with an exclamation expressive of dismay, and almost of horror.

There, spread before him, was a sight, beautiful, even
ravishing had it only been displayed in its proper place,
but which became an object of intensest aversion to him
as a moral young bachelor when found in his trunk
and his chamber, for there lay lovely dresses, neatly
folded and carefully packed, as their fair owner had
arranged them for her journey,—dresses which gave
promise of most bewitching toilets,—when worn by
their rightful owner,—delicate *lingerie*, dainty bonnets : in short, all the paraphernalia of a costly feminine wardrobe,—this was the sight revealed to Warren's horrified gaze when he threw back the lid of
what he had until now believed to be his trunk,
filling his soul with consternation while language con-

tained no words capable of expressing his dismay. Manifestly there must be a mistake! Yet on the surface everything appeared to be all right. His trunk had been new when he left New York; he had purchased it expressly for this journey. The travel stains and scars, won in many an honorable conflict with the baggage-men, showed that this was all true of the cabinet of horrors before him. There were initials on each end corresponding exactly to those which he had had stencilled on his,—M. H. W., N. Y.

(Oh! why had not kind fate prompted either himself or this young woman to order the name to be painted in full once at least?)

On the surface everything appeared to be all right: in reality all was terribly wrong.

He saw it all now. When he went up-town on reaching Los Angeles to spend the night and talk real estate he ought not to have claimed his baggage and left it in the care of the baggage-master unchecked. He had done this same thing hundreds of times before, but now it had happened once too often. Some young woman had manifestly done likewise; some young woman having the same initials as himself and also owning as exact a duplicate of his trunk. So it came about that they had made an exchange, and each was the loser by it. These things were worse than useless to him: he could not wear them; he could not give them away. He had no wife, no sister, not even a sister-in-law upon whom he could bestow this unlucky windfall; while, were he to attempt to offer it, costly as the wardrobe was, to any young lady of his acquaintance—he dared not picture to himself the indignant scorn with which such an offer would be rejected.

Then, his heart was moved with compassion as he pictured to himself the anguish with which his unhappy fellow-victim would look upon her new possessions. If he was overwhelmed, what must her sufferings be? What sobs and exclamations indicative of the intensest misery must burst from her fair lips! (For, of course she must be young and pretty.)

If these dainty and lovely things were worse than useless to him, what could she do with the trousers and coats and vests fated to meet her shocked and terrified eyes when she opened the trunk which he had packed; and that meerschaum-pipe, that bottle of muscatel, that other bottle of brandy carefully stored away in case of need? He closed the lid and turned away with a groan of keenest suffering; the picture was too harrowing.

What was to be done?

California is a large State through which to search for one young woman of whom nothing is known beyond the single fact that on a given day in January, 1888, she was at the Southern Pacific station in Los Angeles, and there made an exchange of trunks with a young man; and that her initials, like his, are M. H. W.

She might even then be in Ventura; she might be in Santa Barbara; she might have gone on to San Francisco; she might be anywhere for all he knew. Possibly she had taken the train to go back to New York, though, considering the season of the year, this was not at all probable.

What was to be done? He could not advertise. It was not a matter that would bear too much ventilation. His soul writhed in anguish at the thought of the snickering inquiries that would be made of him by all his friends if this story should ever get back to New York.

Then, what could be done? Manifestly nothing, for the night at least, except to go to bed and make the best of the matter. So to bed he went, to dream about the problem and wait to see what solution the next day would offer.

CHAPTER II.

It was late when Warren woke on the following morning, his troubles not having weighed upon his mind sufficiently to rob him of a sound and refreshing sleep during the night. After dressing he went to the bay-window, raised the shade, and looked out. An exclamation of delight escaped him. "What a magnificent panorama!" he exclaimed. And truly the view well deserved the name he gave it, for this is what he saw.

The rain had ceased during the night, and the sun, now two hours high, was shining in a sky perfectly cloudless, and blue with that depth found nowhere except in Italy, the Riviera, and Southern California.

The street upon which the house where he had taken lodgings stood wound around the foot-hills nearly half-way to their summit, and the whole city of Ventura lay spread out before him. The broad, straight streets ran from the foot-hills down to the beach and were lined on either side with trees, their rich green foliage gently waving in the soft, refreshing breeze.

The houses, each with its lawn and garden filled with roses, heliotrope, and geraniums, all in full bloom, were shaded with orange-, fig-, and palm-trees; while many of them were almost buried under dense masses of flowering vines.

In the midst of the city two gigantic date-palms

2   13

lifted their venerable heads high above all else; while beyond lay the ocean, its waves sparkling in the sunshine, the surf breaking on the shore with a musical roar.

About twenty miles out in the ocean lay the two islands of Anacapa and Santa Cruz, not seeming half that distance in the clear atmosphere, which brought out every formation of mountain and coast-line with such minute distinctness.

At his feet the old mission of the Holy Cross reared its massive yellow walls, ugly yet quaint and picturesque, though its effect was marred by the new shingled roof with which, in the rage for modern improvements, the parish authorities have replaced the old tiled roof of Father Junipero Serra's times.

Beyond the old mission, and to the left, a long black wharf ran far out into the ocean, at the side of which lay a schooner discharging a cargo of lumber, while a steamer was just making its way from it out into the ocean, gracefully rolling to the motion of the waves, its brass work gleaming in the sunlight like burnished gold.

Going now to the west window, the sight which met his gaze from there was fully as beautiful, and Warren was almost tempted to pronounce it even more lovely than the first. A bend in the coast once more brought the ocean into full view. Back, miles from the city, but looking almost within easy walking distance, lay the Sierra Madre Mountains, bare, wrinkled, and old looking, their summits crowned with snow. Between the mountains and the city lay the foot-hills, rising in higher and higher peaks as they neared the mountains, their sides green with vegetation and their tops crested with groups of live-oaks. From the beach there ran a broad, straight avenue lined on either side with pretty cottage houses embowered in ornamental shrubbery, holding its course straight on to the distant mountains until, winding around among the hills, it became lost to sight.

Beyond the avenue lay the Ventura River, glistening in the sunlight like a silver thread as it hastened onward to mingle its waters with the ocean. On one of the hills back of the city and immediately above the house a Chinaman was ploughing with two white horses, while the steep sides of all the neighboring hills were already green with young vegetables and grain. Altogether the scene was like a glimpse into fairy-land to one who, like Warren, had only a few days before been among the snow-covered hills of the East; but even fairy-land will not long charm the thoughts of a young man blessed with good health and a strong appetite who has yet to breakfast, and whose mind is preoccupied with the attempt to solve a difficulty which, like that in which Warren now found himself involved, was more vexatious than serious.

During the ten minutes required to walk the short distance lying between his lodgings and the Hôtel Anacapa, where he had arranged to board, Warren's thoughts were busily occupied with the absurd predicament in which he found himself placed. What was to be done?

All through his breakfast he asked himself this same question, but without finding himself any nearer to a satisfactory answer.

"I wonder if Mitchell is here yet?" he said to himself, as he made his way into the hotel-office. "He is due, and I sincerely hope that he has arrived. It will do no harm to ask."

"Yes," the clerk replied to whom Warren proposed his question, Mr. Mitchell and his family had been at the house since Christmas. They were all of them in, or at least he thought so; would he like to see them? If he would go into the parlor for a moment word would be given them right away.

"I will thank you to take my card to Mr. Mitchell," Warren replied. "I will call on the ladies some other time."

Warren had hardly seated himself by the glowing fire cheerily burning in the fireplace of the parlor of the Anacapa before his friend was with him, overjoyed at the arrival of an old and intimate acquaintance to be a fellow-sojourner with himself and his family among strangers and in a strange land.

"Well, Warren," Mitchell exclaimed, shaking him heartily by the hand as he spoke, "I am right glad to see you; I had almost begun to give you up and think that you had changed your mind about coming at all."

"Oh, no; I did not come out as you did, merely on a pleasure-trip, so I needed more time than you in preparations, married man though you are," Warren replied.

Mitchell looked doubtfully into his friend's face for a moment, then replied by a question.

"You don't mean to tell me that you have caught this real-estate fever?" he asked.

Warren laughed, though a little uneasily, and as though he was not, after all, perfectly satisfied with himself.

"Yes, Mitchell, I have determined to see if I can manage the boom," he answered.

No two men could be more unlike than these friends. Warren was still on the sunny side of thirty, and in person was slender, athletic, and above the medium height. Mitchell, on the contrary, was much nearer forty than thirty, and while he was not positively ugly, he was very far from being a handsome man. He labored under the threefold disadvantage of being too stout for his height, too bald for his years, and too near-sighted for his own comfort or that of his friends.

Warren was quick to learn and as quick to forget; he was always on the watch for some new enterprise and was constantly on the search for some new excitement, and it was these traits in his character which had brought him away from New York in the height of the season to become a speculator in Southern California.

Mitchell, on the other hand, was slow to learn, but when he once had mastered an idea it became his property; it was always at his command when he wanted to use it, and his judgment was, from this fact, highly valued by all who knew him. Warren, in short, was "a good fellow," Mitchell was a valuable man. Unlike as they were these two men were the closest of friends, each finding in the other points which supplied his own deficiencies.

Mitchell's face expressed the gravest disapproval as he listened to Warren's announcement of this new

business project in which he was already embarked.
Wiping his glasses he put them on again, and sat
thoughtfully looking at his friend through them without speaking.

"What is it, Mitchell?" Warren asked, shifting uneasily under his friend's scrutiny. "What are you
staring at? Do you see some great change in me since
we last met,—symptoms of early decline, or the
like?"

"No, not that. I was looking for wildness in the
eyes. I gathered from your conversation that you
were threatened with insanity; it may be incipient im-
becility, however," Mitchell answered.

"Come, be reasonable," Warren said, impatiently.
"You have always been preaching to me about wasting
my time and letting my abilities run to seed, and all
that; and the very moment that I tell you that I have
come to California for the purpose of going to work,
you call me an idiot and a lunatic."

"Warren, as a truthful man, do you mean to say
that in turning speculator you are following my advice?" Mitchell asked, his tone almost severe.

"Not in the letter, perhaps, as you simply told me
to put out my shingle and go practising law, and did
not mention any other pursuit in connection with it; but
as all the lawyers out here combine real-estate broker-
age with the practice of their profession, you see that I
am not straying so very far from the straight and narrow way marked out for me by your wisdom, after
all," Warren answered.

Mitchell shook his head. "Hardly," he said.
"This present real-estate craze is something like the

gold excitement of '49, only it won't last quite as long.
Like that craze it is going to do a tremendous sight of
mischief, while it will do some good by turning attention to this country, whose advantages in soil and
climate are all that they are said to be, even in the
prospectus of the wildest speculator. Meanwhile, a
few gulls are going to be plucked, and I am sorry that
you are to be one of them; however, it is too late to
talk of that now; your arrangements are all made, of
course?"

"Yes; I entered into partnership before I left
home," Warren answered.

"Who with?" Mitchell asked.

"Glenn. I don't suppose you ever heard of him,"
Warren answered.

"No; I don't pay much attention to real estate, but
how did you arrange it?"

"Through a mutual friend who recommended us to
one another, and we arranged the partnership by cor-
respondence," Warren explained.

"Well, I hope that you won't get fleeced too badly,"
was the only answer he vouchsafed; then abruptly
dropping the subject, he said, "Let me call the ladies."

"Not yet," Warren hastily returned. "To tell the
truth, I have begun my life out here with a very unpleasant experience, and I want to talk it over with
you."

"All right; I am altogether at your service,"
Mitchell answered, again sitting down, wondering
what misfortune his friend's speculative mania could
have brought on him so early in his career.

Warren blushed, looked very foolish, then began

with an air of desperation : "To tell the simple facts of the case, and this is what I want to do, I have got to put myself completely into your power. Now, Mitchell, if I give you my confidence as fully as this, I want you to promise not to betray me even to your wife."

What had his friend been doing? Had he already swindled some one so outrageously before he had been twenty-four hours in the business, or had even seen his first sunset in Ventura, that he was involved in a serious lawsuit so soon? It was not at all like Warren : he was a straightforward and honorable fellow, and it did not seem possible that even his craze for speculation could have so altogether transformed him. As these thoughts flashed through Mitchell's mind he once more took off his glasses, wiped them, put them on, and stared hard at Warren, saying in a tone into which he threw only half the astonishment he felt, "In the name of goodness, what have you been up to?"

"Nothing, Mitchell, nothing at all," Warren hastily replied. "It was not my fault; it was not anybody's fault; there is no blame anywhere. I am in a ridiculous scrape all the same, though, and if you give me away to your wife I know it will get out, and I shall be a laughing-stock to the end of my days." And again Warren shuddered as he thought of the anxious inquiries concerning the state of his wardrobe with which he would be greeted on his return to New York by all his acquaintances in case Mitchell should consider the joke too good to keep ; while it required only a slight exercise of the imagination on his part to picture to himself the conscious yet amused glances which his young lady friends would cast upon him; for of course through husbands and brothers the "joke" would get to their knowledge, as such things always do.

"I give you my word, Warren, that if you have anything to tell me which ought to be kept, I will treat it as a professional secret," Mitchell answered. And drawing his chair close to that of his friend, so that no one could overhear them in case a third party should enter the parlor, Warren proceeded to unfold his tale of woe.

At first a look of blank amazement overspread Mitchell's face; then his eyes twinkled merrily as he listened, while his sides shook with suppressed laughter, but not a sound escaped his lips. When Warren concluded his story he rose from his chair saying, "I will be as silent as the grave, old fellow, you may depend upon me. Not one word of this affair will I breathe to a living soul. But let me call the ladies now."

"Wait! You have not advised me what to do or how to act," Warren protested. Mitchell merely laughed. The absurdity of his friend's situation seemed to impress him more forcibly than its unpleasantness, and he remained most aggravatingly unsympathetic.

"Oh, your case is by no means desperate. If worst comes to worst you can buy yourself another outfit, you know," Mitchell heartlessly answered.

Warren began to be very angry with his friend; he had never known him to be so cold-blooded and indifferent before; it was not like his usual self at all, and he could not understand his manner.

"That has nothing to do with the case at all," Warren answered, showing his vexation both in voice and manner. "What I want to know is, what am I to do with those confounded traps up in my room? I can't let them be seen."

Again Mitchell laughed. "Oh, I am not ready with my advice on that score yet," he answered. "Just be patient and I will help you out of the scrape in some way, trust me for that. But I am going to call the ladies. You have never met my wife's sister, I believe?"

"No; I have always been deprived of that pleasure by some adverse fate. Is she with you now?"

"Yes. We left her to visit a friend of hers in Los Angeles and she came on to join us last evening. You and she both chose a fine day for travelling. And, by the way, you came up on the same train, so you must have seen each other."

"That does not follow, for I rode the entire distance in the smoker; but I wish I had known she was on the train."

"Under those circumstances you probably did not see her, for she seldom travels in that car; but excuse me for a moment," Mitchell rejoined. After an absence of ten minutes he returned accompanied by a very pretty girl, whose dark eyes, at once soft and brilliant, were the certain indications of an amiable disposition, keen wit, and high spirits.

"My wife is not in, so you will have to excuse her; I have brought her sister, however. Miss Wade, my friend Mr. Warren," he said, introducing them.

As they bowed in acknowledgment he maliciously

added, " I find that each one of you rejoices in the possession of initials to which the other can also establish a claim, while each of you is made unhappy by a windfall as unwelcome as it is useless to you ; now, I have promised not to say a word about this business, and I would die before I would break faith with either one of you, so not a single syllable shall escape my lips about it, you may trust me implicitly on that score, but I will just leave you to arrange matters to suit yourselves. May you be prosperous and happy !" And with these words he left the room chuckling audibly, while Warren and Miss Wade stood looking at each other in embarrassed silence.

CHAPTER III

MANY years ago, when making a pedestrian tour, I came to a river of considerable width and decidedly deep which it was necessary for me to cross. There was no bridge, I could not swim, while it would have been very inconvenient for me to adopt that method of transit even had I understood the science (so I must call it, I suppose, now that it is dignified by "professors"). The only means of crossing open to me, so far as I could see, was a huge tree which had fallen across the stream and whose top was apparently firmly held by two trees standing side by side upon the opposite bank, between which it had lodged in falling. In this I had found, as I supposed, a secure bridge ready at my need. But alas for human calculations! Thinking only of a possible danger more or less remote, I neglected to attend to the actual perils close at hand. The fallen tree was anchored to the bank on which I was standing only by the frailest of roots, and it needed nothing but my added weight to plunge both my bridge and myself into the water, from which I struggled out a miserable wretch; wet and muddy as to my person, wrathful and unhappy as to my mind.

Now Warren, when he found himself confronted by Miss Wade, and plunged by Mitchell into the worst aspect of those very difficulties out of which he was trusting to this friend to deliver him; when he saw

24

that he was ruthlessly abandoned to extricate himself from this plight as best he could, felt very much as I did when I found myself betrayed by my tree many years ago. Morally he was very much in the same plight in which I then found myself physically,—he was almost helpless, miserable, and abject.

Miss Wade stood before him without a word, her face burning with confusion ; while Warren, in his turn, for the first time in his life, found himself alone in the company of a pretty and interesting young lady to whom he had not a single word to say. All this time, however, that he stood in speechless embarrassment before his charming companion, he felt a strong inward conviction that when he once more found himself alone with Mitchell he would be at no loss for words, but would be able to express himself freely and forcibly in regard to his friend's behavior on this occasion.

Deep as was his sympathy for himself in this embarrassing situation, Warren's compassion for Miss Wade was even more profound, and he felt a sincere anxiety to lessen her confusion and relieve her unhappiness ; so, gathering together as many of his faculties as surprise and embarrassment had left under his immediate control, he said,—

"I am most happy to meet you, Miss Wade. Indeed, I have so often heard your name mentioned by your sister and Mr. Mitchell that I already look upon you almost as an old acquaintance, though I wish that my friend had arranged for our first meeting under circumstances which would have made the pleasure attended by no sense of pain."

"I sympathize with you cordially in that sentiment,

Mr. Warren," Miss Wade answered, with a light in her eyes which gave promise that Mr. Mitchell would find his "joke" bringing upon his head the full weight of her displeasure. "I think that my brother-in-law has shown himself less than friendly to you and certainly less than kind to me."

Warren placed a chair for her, and as she seated herself he went to the fireplace, and resting one foot on the fender he hesitated a moment, as though in doubt as to what he should say next. The simple truth is, that never in his life had he been so thoroughly uncomfortable; while never before, since the boyish and awkward days of his dancing-school miseries, had the society of an attractive and handsome young lady possessed the power of making him thoroughly and unspeakably wretched.

"Of course I understand what Mitchell intended," he said after a moment's silence; "as my intimate friend of many years' standing and your brother-in-law, he took the advantage of the close relations existing between himself and each one of us to derive amusement for himself at our expense, without stopping to consider that you and I are perfect strangers to one another."

"There you are naming the very point he should not have forgotten, Mr. Warren," Miss Wade answered, her strong indignation against her brother-in-law appearing in the tones of her voice.

"Very true; and I shall make every effort to convince him of the fact," Warren replied.

Again there was silence. Evidently nothing was to be gained by longer postponing the evil day. It was just as evident that Miss Wade could not first broach the matter which must be discussed between them. As that which must be done had best be done quickly, Warren at once plunged into the very midst of the subject.

"Miss Wade," he said, "it seems that you and I bear the same initials. While I feel honored by the fact, it has its inconvenient as well as—to me, that is—pleasing features; and it has placed us at the present moment in very embarrassing relations to one another. I am, as of course you are aware, possessed of property belonging to you, while you have accidentally obtained my belongings. On·my return to my room I will at once restore your property to you, and will, at your convenience, relieve you of what must have been to you an annoying and distressing charge. And permit me, Miss Wade, to most sincerely express my regret for the distress that my mistake has caused you, and I hope you will pardon the blunder."

Miss Wade blushed crimson. Without raising her eyes, she replied, "I thank you, Mr. Warren. The adventure must have been as annoying to you as to me, and in committing the mistake I do not doubt that we are equally responsible, while neither one of us is in the least to blame."

Warren bowed. "It is good of you to say so," he answered; then at once abruptly. changing a subject painful to both, he went on : "In California the one absorbing topic of conversation is the country and its wonderful climate; that is, among the men at least. I gather from what Mitchell says that you have been here long enough now to be no longer reckoned among the new-comers, so perhaps this topic no longer possesses interest to you."

Mollie began to feel more at her ease now that that wretched business was disposed of, so she laughed as she answered, "I have been in the State almost three months now. Were I intending to make it my home here that would give me the right to call myself an old Californian, would it not?"

Warren laughed in his turn as he replied, "That is the law, I believe. But custom also prescribes that a good Californian should stand loyally by his section : he must never by any chance admit that he can possibly be ignorant upon any topic concerning the country, its interests or its possibilities : he must always proclaim to the world· the richness of the soil, the inexhaustible mineral resources, and the glories of the climate in his section ; he must carefully keep back any possible disadvantages that may exist, however slight ; and last, but by no means least, if a new-comer, he must evade the question as to how long he has been here,—all these are the qualities of a good Californian, and I am already making them my own."

For the first time during their interview Miss Wade lifted her eyes to his face ; now, meeting his with a swift glance, half of inquiry, half of amusement, she answered, "You seem to understand the customs of the people here thoroughly. You have been more profoundly observant of their character and prejudices in your residence of twenty-four hours than I in my three months' sojourn. Do you intend to make Ventura your home?"

"I have not decided ; indeed, my answer to that

question will altogether depend upon circumstances, and that I may fairly discuss that topic with you I must begin by making a confession and admitting that I have been an alarmingly idle man," Warren replied.

"The old, old story of great gifts and rich endowments allowed to run to waste : is that your meaning ?" she asked, again glancing at him swiftly.

Again Warren laughed, but this time a trifle uneasily, for he felt a painful suspicion that he was being quizzed.

"I can hardly say that," he answered. "But I do mean that, since stern necessity did not spur me on and compel me to work, I have fallen into the long procession of do-nothings. However, here I am in California, and, strangest of all, filled with a strong desire to become industrious, and actually embarked in business. So I suppose this will be my home, if I succeed. It is a change from New York and my life there, is it not ?"

"A decided change. What has worked so great a miracle ?" she said, answering his question by another.

"Oh, that great worker of all modern miracles, California and the interest it is exciting in the East. You are an Easterner ; is not my explanation complete ?"

"It is perfect !" she answered, clasping her hands in pretended enthusiasm. "I cannot imagine any less powerful agent changing a New York society man into a Western pioneer. But frankly, I do not wonder at your coming, neither shall I wonder if you stay. One hears so much about the wonders of Southern California in these days that one wishes to see her marvels

3*

for one's self. Then, when one gets here, there is such
a fascination about the scenery, the climate, and the
free and joyous out-door life, that one wishes to stay.
The glamour of the tropics is over it all."

Decidedly he did like the girl. Although their in-
troduction had been so very much out of the common at
the first that it had taken all possibility of pleasure
out of their meeting, he now felt thoroughly convinced
that her acquaintance was well worth all the distress
their first meeting had cost him. She was a very
bright girl; she was thoroughly independent; and as
he expressed it in his conscious masculine superiority,
"she had ideas."

At that moment the door opened and Mrs. Mitchell
hurried into the parlor. A fresh, breezy little woman
with a bright and pleasant face; no one, from her
manner, would have thought that at that very moment
Mitchell was sitting up-stairs in his room thinking
with hardened impenitence upon a severe lecture from
her lips concerning his shameless and unfeeling conduct towards these two young people who, above all
others in the world, had the greatest claims upon his
consideration. Greeting Warren with the cordial free-
dom of an old friend she said, "At last you have come,
and you cannot imagine how glad we are to see you,
or how much good it will do us to have you here.
And to think that you are actually going to stay! I
am glad that you and Mollie have at last become acquainted; and of course, like all the other lotos-eaters,
you are thinking and talking of nothing but California
and its wonders."

Mollie and Warren glanced at one another, again

their eyes met for an instant, and both laughed as he answered, "I plead guilty ; but let it be my all-sufficient excuse that I have found this the one theme not only in the State but among all the travellers coming to it."

"Yes," Miss Wade interposed, "as Effie says, we Americans are now seeing the old Homeric myth illustrated in real life. We are all of us either lotoseaters, or else we are hungering for an opportunity to taste the fated leaf."

Warren rose from his chair, and going to the window looked out over the picture displayed before him, saying, "Is not this enough to make one forget home, and country, and his father's house? It is like living in an atmosphere of poetry. But you must visit me in my domicile, for I think my outlook surpasses even this, for it takes in the mountains as well as the city, and the ocean."

"Where are you residing?" Mrs. Mitchell asked.

"On Poli Street, with Mrs. Elkins. I wish you to know her, for she interested me immediately on meeting her. I know I shall find her a study in human nature, what is technically called a character, you know."

"Why, Mr. Warren, you are planning for a busy life, are you not? combining the pursuit of moral anatomy with dealings in real estate. From what I had seen of Californians I had formed the idea that the law of their life was to combine the least possible amount of business with the greatest possible amount of pleasure ; but you seem to be reversing this law,—unless, perhaps, scientific research be recreation to you !" Miss Wade exclaimed.

Warren glanced at her keenly with a renewal of the uneasy feeling that he was being quizzed. He wished that he knew whether the girl were laughing at him or not, though he strongly suspected that she was; his suspicions were immediately strengthened by his detecting the glance which her sister cast at her, half amused, half reproachful, as she said, in answer to Warren's remark,—

"What did you mean by calling your landlady a character, Mr. Warren? I hope, for your own peace of mind, that you are not lodging with one of those horrible specimens of eccentricity and disagreeableness who usually receive that title."

"Oh, no, not quite so bad as that; she is a California Yankee," he answered, drawing on his gloves as he spoke.

"You must be more explicit," she said; "that leaves us in even deeper darkness than before. What is a California Yankee?"

"I cannot say that I am ready with an exact definition, though the idea is clear to my own mind," Warren answered. "My landlady will have to serve as an illustration, therefore. She is a native daughter of the Golden West, but she possesses the true Yankee physiognomy. She is very tall, but thin and active; and even with my short acquaintance I can see that she suffers under a continual apprehension that some one is anxious to infringe upon her rights and sacred prerogatives; all of these traits are characteristic of the Yankee. So, you see, although I am a stranger in a strange land, being by birth a Yankee myself, I find that she makes me feel quite at home."

"We will come and see for ourselves, Mr. Warren. Must you go? Do come and see us every day," Mrs. Mitchell entreated.

"We shall meet at the table every day, for this is to be my boarding-place," Warren answered. "And as for further visiting,—well, as Miss Wade says, I am to be a busy man; but where is Mitchell?"

"You will find him up-stairs," Mrs. Mitchell answered.

Taking leave of the ladies, Warren went to his friend's room for the purpose of pouring forth upon his too jovial head the full contents of the vials of his wrath. He found upon analyzing his feelings that his anger was by no means as fierce as it had been: his fury had been greatly appeased by his pleasant visit, and Miss Wade's acquaintance was certainly well worth whatever annoyance he had experienced in its making. Yes, she certainly was a very pretty girl and he liked her very much: he hoped that she liked him.

"What do you think of our friend, Mollie?" Mrs. Mitchell asked after he was gone.

"Why, to tell the truth, I had not thought about him at all. Is it necessary that I should?" she answered, indifferently.

Her sister was inclined to be vexed with her for turning her words in this way.

"What a girl you are, Mollie!" she answered. "You know perfectly well what I mean. I hope that, as we like him so much, you will be good friends with him also."

"Oh, so far as that is concerned, I do not dislike him at all. He is well enough in his way, like every

c

other commonplace young man of the period," Mollie answered, still supremely indifferent, and apparently a trifle bored by the subject under discussion.

"It was a perfect shame of John Addison to treat you two as he did," Mrs. Mitchell went on, now becoming vehement in language and gesture as she touched upon the injury done to her sister and her friend.

Miss Wade blushed, but answered very quietly, "Of course it was painfully embarrassing to us both ; but Mr. Warren was not at all to blame, and he behaved very handsomely. As far as any friendship between us is concerned, that will altogether depend upon his merits, and the peculiar circumstances of our meeting will not affect that in the least."

"Certainly not," Mrs. Mitchell assented, although she knew perfectly well that her sister was not at all like other women if these did not influence her mind against the man. Then she resumed the subject, answering her sister's criticism of Warren, "As for Mr. Warren being simply a young man of the period, he certainly is not that. I admit that he has never done anything in his profession, because he has not felt the necessity ; but if circumstances were to call out what is in him, you would certainly find him more than an average young man, and the simple fact that he has come out here for the purpose of going to work shows you that he does amount to something, does it not ?"

"I don't call his enterprise *work*, Effie," Miss Wade answered, with a contemptuous curl of the lip. "It looks to me very much like gambling; simply a scheme devised by a rich young man to increase his fortune without doing anything to earn it."

"Are you sure you are not prejudiced, Mollie?"
Mrs. Mitchell asked, wishing to awaken her sister to a
realization of the injustice she was doing Warren by
the sweeping accusation she had brought against the
young man and his motives, but too wise to deepen her
antagonism by discussing the point.

"Prejudiced?" Miss Wade replied, as though surprised beyond expression at the very suspicion of such
a thing. "Certainly, I am not prejudiced in the least.
Why should I be? I see no reason for prejudice on
my part, since I know so very little about the man;
and I can find no sufficient reason why I should have
any opinion about him either good or bad. Or, for
that matter, why I should feel any interest in him now
that I have recovered my property," she added, with a
laugh.

It would do no good to press the argument any further; this was a matter which time, and time alone,
could deal with,—provided it ever were successfully
dealt with. Mrs. Mitchell saw this, and wisely dismissed the whole subject, simply saying in reply,
"Very well, Mollie, we will leave it that way, then."

CHAPTER IV.

It was late in the evening before Warren returned to his lodgings. As the night was perfect, the moon being at the full, and not a cloud even so large as a man's hand was visible in the heavens, he had intentionally taken the longest route to his room for the sake of walking along the beach and watching the ocean by moonlight. His way home led him through the Plaza, which was a good-sized plot of ground originally intended for a public park, but as it still remained unimproved it was never used, and very seldom was even crossed except as a short cut between the intersecting streets.

Warren was sauntering along enjoying the pleasant evening and inhaling the soft air, fragrant with the odor of roses and orange-blossoms, when the sound of voices made him aware that he was never less alone than when alone; though in this instance, at least, he was compelled to interpret the words in an entirely different sense from that in which the great (and one must also fear, conceited) originator of the saying intended.

Looking across the Plaza in the direction of the voices, Warren saw a young man and woman seated upon the trunk of a eucalyptus-tree which had been felled in order to make way for further improvements; and so deeply were they interested in one another that they were altogether oblivious of all the world beside.

86

In the young man Warren at once recognized no less a personage than the son of his landlady, Jake Elkins by name; an ungainly, overgrown, good-natured fellow of twenty-two years or thereabouts; while the girl's soft voice and peculiar accent proved her to be a native daughter of the soil, either of Mexican or Spanish-American blood.

A more hopeless hero for a romance than our friend Jake Elkins it would be difficult to imagine. By all the laws of romantic art, a hero, to be interesting, should be as graceful as Apollo, while he should also be possessed of dove-like, melting eyes. Now our friend Jake had neither of these attributes. If he could be fittingly compared to any of the classic heathen deities, the most partial of his friends would have been compelled to admit that he had far more of Silenus than of Apollo in his physical appearance. Let it be a sufficient description of his person to say that he was twenty-two years of age, and that he weighed two hundred pounds; while as for his eyes, they were certainly not dove-like, and they had never learned the art of melting.   .

Yet this unheroic hero was endowed with one heroic attribute at least, for it was clear to the most unsympathetic observer that he was most devotedly in love. A single glance in the direction of the young couple was sufficient to reveal this fact to Warren; and as he walked along, this love-scene in real life called to his mind a love-scene he had just been reading of in one of the last novels written by the " Prophetess of Passion," and that so forcibly that he burst into a laugh.

There, the fair young authoress describes her hero as

flinging himself upon his knees before the heroine and pressing "his lips now on one foot, now on the other; then, kneeling up, he kissed her dress, her knees, her waist, her arms," and last of all, their lips "clung into a kiss."

"Could Jake's two hundred pounds of humanity be successfully cast at the feet of his Iberian divinity?" Warren asked of himself, as he sauntered up the steep street towards his lodgings, idly switching the heads from the wild-flowers with his cane as he slowly walked along. Again he laughed to himself as he pictured Jake's ungainly form "kneeling up" before his pretty Spanish sweetheart; not that he knew what "kneeling up" might be, or how it was done; but whatever it was, it could not very well fail of being something peculiarly interesting in the present instance.

The next morning, on his way down to his office, he met the actor in last night's love-scene also going out; and, having already become fast friends, he greeted him with, "By the way, Jake, have you no front gate handy about here?"

Jake looked at him with a puzzled expression in his honest eyes as he answered,—

"We took ours down when the street was graded. Why? d'ye think the place 'd look better if 'twas put back?"

"Oh, that is not what I was thinking of, Jake," Warren answered. "My interest in that useful article lies deeper than any question of mere appearances. I was thinking, as I saw you last night in the Plaza, that a front gate in a private door yard would be far more æsthetic as well as far more secure from the intrusions of heartless listeners than a eucalyptus log in the public park of a city ; that's all."

Jake blushed, looked uncomfortable, and seemed more unheroic than ever in his confusion. At last, with an air of desperate determination, as though he felt obliged to say something but did not exactly know what would best meet the circumstances of the case, he asked, "Did you see us, Mr. Warren ?"

"See you?" Warren answered, as though astonished at the question. "Why, my dear Jake, you did not suppose, did you, that your good angel was going to strike every passer-by with temporary blindness in order that you and your fair maid might do your courting in the Plaza unobserved by those whom business or other necessity might call that way ?"

"Why, no," Jake said, kicking the ground with his right foot and burying his hands deep in his trousers-pockets. "I didn't count on nothin' except that nobody 'd cut across there last night. It's the last place in town folks ever go to."

"True, it is not, just at present, an especially attractive place," Warren answered. "Still, it is public property ; and, consequently, it is not just the place in which to do your courting, as even your confiding nature must see, Jake, after a little reflection. Will not papa furnish lights and a parlor? If not, I fall back on my original suggestion ; and, as your friend, I strongly advise a front gate. Not that I ever tried one myself ; but it is so cordially endorsed by popular testimony that I feel very confident that that which receives such hearty commendation from all

quarters *must* possess peculiar merits. Don't you think
so, Jake ?"

Jake looked up as Warren addressed this last question to him, then looked down again, still kicking the
ground, as he answered, "Seems like you're pokin' fun
at me, Mr. Warren."

"Perish the thought !" Warren answered, lighting
a cigar as he spoke. "I like you, Jake, and I am
simply acting as a friend and giving you friendly
advice. Whatever other ill-considered thing you may
do, don't, for heaven's sake, intrude your love-affairs on
the public gaze. They ought to be kept strictly private ; and the public is sure to be unsympathetic, and
also feels painfully in the way when brought into the
presence of two lovers, as I was last night. That is
what I mean, Jake, and I never was more in earnest in
my life. Have a cigar ?"

Jake accepted the proffered treat, but did not feel it
at all necessary to thank the giver, and said, "Goin'
down street, Mr. Warren ?"

"Yes."

"I'll just walk down with you ; and I don't mind
if I tell you about it."

When he began this conversation Warren had not
intended to become the repository of Jake's love-secrets ;·
but, as he had told him, he had merely intended to give
him a hint that, if he were in the habit of choosing
the Plaza for his courting, he was doing it a little too
publicly. As he had said, though, he liked the young
fellow ; and when Jake offered him his confidence,
Warren accepted it with the frankness which was a
part of his nature.

"Just as you choose, Jake," he answered; "I'll keep faith with you, though I cannot promise to act as a counsellor. I fear I should not make a good one were I to try to act the part, as I have had no experience in such matters, and I don't think my advice would be worth much were I to give it."

"I ain't just askin' for advice, Mr. Warren," Jake said, in response to this caution. "I don't see no way you could help me if you was to try. Seein' 's you know so much, though, I'd like you to know the rest; so I'll tell you if you don't mind listenin'."

"Not the least in the world, Jake, if you don't mind telling. And if you should see any way in which I can help you, command me," Warren answered, knocking the ashes from his cigar.

"I will that!" Jake answered, gratefully. "You bet I'll remember. Now, you see the business 's this way. She is Camilla Carballo." (Jake did not consider it necessary to further define the young lady than by the feminine pronoun.) "Her father's a rich old Spaniard here in town, and they've lived here forever, I reckon. They don't like me because I'm a Yankee; my mother won't let me speak of her 'cause she ain't."

"In your case, the course of true love is dammed by a double difficulty, isn't it?" Warren interjected.

"You bet!" Jake answered.

"And the cruelty of your respective parents is the cause of your wandering about and taking refuge in public parks and highways and in dens and caves of the earth, instead of doing your courting in the less romantic but far more comfortable parlor of papa's mansion?" Warren again remarked.

4*

"You bet!" Jake again assented. "If I was to go there, old Carballo would fire me out of the house and set the dog on me."

"H—m!" commented Warren. "The parental opposition could not well be more forcibly expressed."

"He'll never give in about me; and the old lady 'll never give in about Camilla; so what is a fellow to do?" Jake disconsolately asked, his mental anguish apparent in every tone of his voice.

There is no form which human unhappiness can assume which receives so little sympathy as that which results from disappointed love; and, as Warren looked at Jake's miserable countenance, he repressed with difficulty a strong desire to laugh, while he saw that his companion was suffering real anguish, absurd as the great hulking fellow looked while mourning over his blighted affections. Jake was devotedly in love; that fact was perfectly clear; and, as Warren looked at him, he thought how unjust is the popular sentiment which ridicules such sorrows, as though there were some excellent joke in a true and pure affection, and its disappointment were, therefore, something to be laughed at; while, were the sufferer laid up with a broken leg, the compassion of these same laughers would be outspoken and sincere, though Jake's sufferings would be no more real in the latter case than they now were; while it was very possible, if not even probable, that they would not do him, in the long run, so much actual injury as would his present disappointment. Was Warren himself feeling the tender influence of this sacred passion? and was this making him more just and generous towards its victims? He did not know himself; and as he did not care to know, he would not examine his feelings in order to ascertain what they were.

"Well, Jake, I am certainly sorry for you," he said, after a few moments of silence on both sides. "Will the girl stand by you, do you think?"

"She'll never marry anybody else!" Jake answered, confidently and proudly.

"You, I take it, will be true to her?" Warren then asked.

"You bet! I'll never look at any other girl," he answered, almost angry at the supposition of possible falseness on his side.

Positively, he did look almost heroic in his indignant repudiation of even the thought of treachery to the girl he loved.

"Well, Jake," Warren answered, "as I told you, I don't consider myself competent to advise in affairs of the heart, having had no experience in such things myself. But, so far as I can see, there is nothing for you to do but simply to wait. Your mother has nothing against the young lady except the fact that she is Spanish, has she?"

"That's all. Says she ain't goin' to have no dirty Greaser callin' her mother. Camilla ain't no Greaser; her family is pure Castilian," Jake answered, indignantly.

"Now, coming to the young lady's family," Warren went on, quietly waiving all those nice distinctions of nationality which were brought up by his companion's protest. "Have they any objection to you? anything in yourself as a man, I mean, of course?"

"Well—I'm a heretic, you know," Jake admitted.

"The whole trouble, then, so far as I can see, grows out of race jealousy and religious prejudice," said Warren.

"I reckon you've hit it," was Jake's answer.

"Then, in my judgment, all you can do is to be patient and wait," said Warren, sagely delivering his opinion. "You are both of you young, and it will not hurt you to wait two or three years yet. I know it will be unpleasant, but it will not hurt you in the least in the end. Just keep up a good heart, and be true to each other, while you must not forget to be also true to yourselves; meanwhile, let things take their course and don't force matters. I think the religious difficulty can be overcome; while the race prejudice seems to me too foolish to be any real obstacle to your happiness. These unreasonable prejudices always grow out of ignorance; and they always disappear when people come to know each other better, and from that simple fact get to liking each other better. So just be patient and wait; and meanwhile remember that I am your friend, and will prove it in any way that I can. Don't be afraid to call upon me at any time. Here is my office, so good-morning."

"Good-by, Mr. Warren. I'm obliged to you," Jake answered, as he went on down the street to the beach with a happier face and a lighter heart than he had carried before for many a day.

CHAPTER V.

THE days passed rapidly into weeks, and March had come, carpeting the hills with brilliant and beautiful wild-flowers. It was just the weather for an excursion, and so it would remain for weeks now: too early for the dust which would come with the long rainless and cloudless summer; too late to be embarrassed by the mountain torrents, swollen by the winter's rains; while the wild-flowers, brought out by these showers, now almost ended for the year, were fast coming to their fullest beauty.

Warren was a firm believer in the joys of a picnic; but in making this admission you must remember that picnics are capable of almost as widely different classifications as are the races of mankind. There is, certainly, very little joy to be found in the average Eastern picnic as it is generally devised and managed. No one likes to be intimately associated for an indefinite number of hours either with the man who has injured him in his business prospects, or—and this is even worse— to be thrown into constant and close contact with the woman who has crushed his dearest and proudest hopes, and be compelled to smile sweetly and converse amiably the while with either of these, whether it be his worst or his dearest foe, under penalty of being looked upon by every one in the party as an uncomfortable person,—one who always makes it a point to be glum and sulky where all beside are agreeable and happy.

45

Nor is the outcome much more pleasant, even when the company is most congenial, for the hitherto gay party to find itself overtaken by a sudden and unexpected shower, with the result that its members are sent home dripping: the ladies cross over their ruined bonnets and dresses; the gentlemen swearing softly to themselves at being deluded into taking part in so imbecile and comfortless an expedition.

But in California, during the proper season, a picnic is an altogether different affair. To begin with, you know that it will not rain. Then, you know that it will be neither too hot for comfort nor too chilly for health, while the scenery will be grandly beautiful; and last of all, if you make any effort to do so, every element of discomfort can be eliminated so far as it is either possible or best to abolish discomfort from our mundane existence. The sum of the matter is, therefore, that every candid person who has made the experiment must admit that it is impossible to spend a season in California without becoming as ardent an admirer of picnics and as enthusiastic an excursionist as was our friend Warren.

He was late that morning at breakfast; and as he entered the dining-room of the Anacapa, he saw that he had the field entirely to himself. Seating himself at the table, he asked the waiter how long it had been since the Mitchells were at breakfast.

"It must have been half an hour ago since they were down," that dignitary replied.

"I wish, after giving my order, you would go to the office and see if they have gone out; and if they have not, tell them that I want to see them and will be up shortly," Warren said, looking over the bill of fare as he spoke.

"Very well, sir," the waiter answered, then disappeared to give the order; and, coming back in an instant, he made his way to the office to fulfil the rest of his commission, his zeal being inspired by his hopes of a fee: hopes which he felt certain were not doomed to disappointment. He returned almost immediately with the message that Mr. Mitchell and all the family were in, and would be happy to see him at his convenience.

Warren thanked him, at the same time rejoicing his heart with a fee which surpassed his wildest expectations, and he departed to bring on Warren's order, the devoted adherent of his benefactor forever.

After finishing his breakfast Warren went at once to the room of his friends, and proceeded to unfold his idea to them. Much to his disgust they received it very coldly indeed, while Mrs. Mitchell was especially firm in her opposition.

"Perhaps it is owing to my ignorance of this country and its customs," she objected. "I admit that I have not taken the same pains to inform myself that you have, Mr. Warren; but really, early March does not seem to me to be the proper time for a picnic."

"Prejudice, simple prejudice!" Warren answered, laughing at her arguments against his great idea. "I fear that you are a good deal of a tenderfoot even yet, or you would recognize the undeniable fact that here the names of the months are used only as a commercial convenience, and as a concession to conventional usage. As for meaning, in this favored land they

possess none at all. Have you consulted your ther-
mometer faithfully while you have been here?"

Mrs. Mitchell was by no means convinced; she
did not, however, attempt to answer his argument,
but contented herself by replying to his question with
a simple "No."

"I thought not," Warren triumphantly answered.
"Your ignorance betrays itself. There is not a single
day in which the mercury does not register seventy
and above; and except for the remote possibility of
a shower it is perfect picnic weather; and this is a
chance you are never free from in your beloved East.
As far as not being warm enough is concerned, one
could go off on such an excursion here in the middle
of January. Try again, Mrs. Mitchell."

"Oh, you need not exult so soon," that lady immediately answered ; "I am not nearly at the end of my list
of objections yet. In the next place, I think it will
be very damp under the trees, and we shall all take
cold eating our lunch there; and I also think it will
be a terrible nuisance to provide and carry provisions;
and I think——"

"Hold, hold, enough of these sad plaints!" Warren
exclaimed, cutting short her objections. "I foresaw
all these difficulties and have carefully provided
against them. Now listen to me, 'Friends one and
all :' *I* do not wish to carry provisions; and for the
world I would not risk the health of that delicate
husband of yours, Mrs. Mitchell, whose sylph-like
form proclaims him to be already a creature belonging
more to the next world than to this."

"Gently, Matt, gently; don't grow personal, or I

shall do you an injury. This too solid flesh is not **a** light matter, and I cannot permit it to be made the subject of merriment," Mitchell said, with a sadly injured air.

Without attempting further sarcasm Warren again resumed the defence of his project. "Very well," he said. "To go into the merits of the case at once, what I propose is that we all go to the Ojai. You have none of you been there; I have. Take my word for it, if you go home without seeing the valley you will lose a visit to one of the most beautiful and delightful places in the whole world. We will simply go for pleasure, and I mean by that, go in light marching order. We will take no provisions, but ride up to the valley; take supper at the Oak Glen Cottages; sleep there, and ride back after breakfast in the morning. How does that strike you for a picnic *à la mode?* What do you say, Miss Wade?" turning to this young lady, who had up to this time taken no part in the discussion.

Mollie laid aside the pretty nothings with which she had been killing time, under the delusion she shared in common with other ladies that doing this was to "work;" and while folding them preparatory to putting them into her basket, she said, in answer to the question Warren had addressed to her, "I don't think you have planned a picnic, Mr. Warren; but I do think you have proposed a very delightful excursion, so I vote that we go."

"Before I commit myself either for or against," said Mitchell, "I want the slight shade of ignorance dissipated which is still obscuring my usually clear per-

c   d   5

ceptions. I think you said something about *riding*, Warren. Do you mean that we shall be conveyed by horses altogether disconnected from vehicles?"

"That was my meaning," Warren answered.

"Calmly, soberly, and while in full possession of all your faculties you made that suggestion?" Mitchell demanded.

"To the best of my knowledge and belief I laid the proposition before you during a lucid interval; however, it may be that you are better calculated to decide that point than I," was Warren's reply.

Mitchell rose from his chair, and standing before Warren so that his ample proportions could not fail to make their full impression upon his friend, he said, "Do I strike you as a man intended by nature to appear before the world in the character of an equestrian?"

"You make altogether too much of your size, Mitchell," Warren answered, impatiently. "Other stout men ride, and why should not you? I don't see any objection on that score."

"I do," Mitchell answered, emphatically. "Never will I place myself on a horse's back, to become an object of scoffing to men and of pity to angels. If I go, I must be dispensed from that part of the programme."

"I see another, and a very important objection which I think it very strange all the rest of you have forgotten. What is to become of our boy, and your little namesake, Mr. Warren?" Mrs. Mitchell inquired, her manner showing very clearly that she regarded this as a difficulty which must be fairly overcome, and would admit of no compromise.

"Can't you leave him here?" Warren indiscreetly suggested.

Mrs. Mitchell gave a little cry of indignant dismay, while both her sister and husband burst into a hearty laugh at her consternation over Warren's proposal and his manifest chagrin at the manner in which it had been received.

"If that is not, for all the world, just like a man!" she exclaimed. "The idea of leaving a baby only two years old in a hotel, among strangers, while his mother goes off on an excursion! Of course that is altogether out of the question. I am surprised at you, Mr. Warren!"

Warren struggled out of the depths of the humiliation into which he had been plunged sufficiently to attempt a defence, and explain the suggestion which the horrified manner of the child's mother too plainly showed she looked upon as stupid if not altogether heartless. So, to show the absence of any cruel intention on his part, he said, "Why, Mrs. Mitchell, the child will not be alone among strangers; his nurse will be with him, and we shall not be gone two days."

"That does not alter the case in the least. Nothing would justify me in going off on such an excursion and leaving my child to the care of a servant among strangers," Mrs. Mitchell answered, with unbending severity.

"Don't say another word, Mr. Warren," Mollie interposed, laughing heartily at her sister's indignation and Warren's air of mingled surprise and humility; for even now he could see nothing so very outrageous in his solution of the difficulty. "If you try to make

any further explanations or suggestions I can see that
you will ruin yourself irretrievably with Effie. I see
no way out of this difficulty, which is really no difficulty, but to let John Addison and Effie go in a
carriage with the boy, while the rest of us ride; or
else, just let the whole matter drop and stay at home.
Now, which had we better do?"

Warren certainly was not going to abandon the
enterprise if this outcome could possibly be avoided.
The prospect of a long ride to the Ojai and back in
Mollie's company was altogether too delightful to be
lightly abandoned. As his eyes met hers, soft, liquid,
and melting, his heart gave a throb of exquisite happiness : it was a delight to him merely to be in her
presence; to know that she was near him; to look
upon her and adore her, even though she knew nothing of his adoration.

"Let it be as you wish," he answered. "I do not
see why the trip cannot be arranged as Miss Wade has
proposed. You can take the boy and go in a carriage;
and, if you and they wish, the Rector and his wife can
go in the same carriage, while the rest of us can ride."

"Now you once more hold your former high place
in my esteem, and I think Effie is also less inclined to
regard you as a monster," Mitchell replied.

Mrs. Mitchell relented at once, and said in answer to
her husband's reference to her,—

"Yes; although the offence was a terrible one, I
attribute it to ignorance and so forgive it. I suppose,
by your suggesting that the Rector and his wife go with
us, you have the party in mind?"

"Yes," Warren answered. "We do not want a

large party. I thought that beside ourselves we would
simply ask my partner and Miss Wade's hotel friend,
Miss Lake; these, with the Rector and his wife, will
make the party large enough, will it not?"

The Rector and his wife were a young couple from
Boston, newly married, who had recently come to the
parish, and had been in the city but a few weeks over
a year.

Mitchell thought the party sufficiently large, and expressed himself delighted with the clerical addition to
their number.

"The Rector and his wife by all means!" he exclaimed. "While the presence of two Bostonians will
lend culture to the company, perhaps their goodness
will act as a counterpoise to the depravity the presence
of two California real-estate dealers will certainly intro-
duce. Now we must decide when we are to go."

"How will the day after to-morrow suit you?"
Warren asked, wholly ignoring his friend's comments.

"All times are alike to us idle tourists, you know,"
Mitchell answered. "You and your partner are the
only men of business to be present; the Rector is the
only man of affairs. If he, Miss Lake, and you two
men of business find that time agreeable to you, it will
be perfectly convenient to us; will it not, ladies?" he
asked, turning to his wife and her sister for the expression of their opinion.

They assented; and thereupon Warren remarked,
"As for the Rector, I have already seen him and asked
if he could go, and on that day, and he has agreed. I
will speak to Miss Lake as I go out; if she happens to
be engaged for that day, we can change the time to meet

her convenience, though I apprehend no danger of postponement on that score, for she is as idle a tourist as yourselves. As for Glenn and myself, our time is not very valuable just at present."

This remark caused Mitchell to look profoundly interested at once. "Is business dull?" he asked.

"A little slack just at present; but then one never has time to work very hard in this country; pleasure before business, you know," Warren answered, trying to evade a direct answer.

But Mitchell was too deeply interested in the issue of his friend's business enterprise to be put off by anything less than a direct and positive refusal on Warren's part to answer any questions; and this he felt certain that he, knowing and respecting his motives in inquiring into the success of this new business venture, would not make.

"You are not doing as well as you expected, I take it?" he next asked, putting a direct question this time.

Warren hesitated a moment as though doubtful whether to answer or not, then as if deciding to give his confidence to his friend, replied, "I did not come this morning to talk business; I shall, however, have something to talk over with you in a few days, after we get things a little more into shape. Just now we are a little dull, but very soon now we shall have something on foot that will make things lively; and even so hardened a sceptic as you will think it worth taking hold of, I feel very sure."

"Ah,—I see," Mitchell replied, meditatively. "Speaking in the language of the country, you are getting up a boom."

"That's it. You've put the whole matter into a nut-shell," Warren answered, while the ladies sat listening with interest, for the subject now being discussed was one entirely new to them, while it was one which was continually mentioned in all the papers, and which formed so absorbing a topic of conversation that no one could be long in Southern California without becoming profoundly interested in it.

Mitchell looked very serious. "You are in it?" he asked.

"Oh, four of us have formed a company," Warren replied.

Mitchell shook his head, his manner plainly showing that he doubted the success of the enterprise, while he further asked, "How much do you expect to make?"

Warren had risen to take his leave, having now completed the arrangements for his excursion, which had been the object of his call; but seeing the doubts entertained by Mitchell of the successful issue of the scheme upon which he had embarked, he replaced his hat upon the table and again sat down, in order to remove all sceptical notions from the mind of his friend as to the brilliant issue awaiting his project, and to defend his own reputation for business sagacity.

"I say once more, that I did not come here this morning to talk business," he replied; "but I will explain what I have already said by telling you that we have taken up a tract of land near this city which we are now laying out into a town site; we are building a reservoir; we shall also make further improvements, and then we shall put it on the market."

Mitchell looked at him with a countenance expres-

sive of the deepest compassion. "Warren," he said,
very gravely, "have you been drawn into this enterprise very deeply?"

Warren was both surprised and piqued by his friend's
serious manner. Although he knew that Mitchell was
altogether out of sympathy with the prevailing land-
craze, he also knew that he was a firm believer in
the future of the country, and he had hoped that, on
general principles, he would at least endorse and support an enterprise which was undertaken fully as much
to develop the country as to enrich its projectors;
Vexed at the manner in which Mitchell persisted in
looking at the project, he made no answer, and Mitchell
went on : "I am not asking this out of curiosity, but
as an old friend. I hope you are not very deeply interested in this matter."

"You need not be at all alarmed; *I* am not. I have
such perfect confidence in the result that I have invested the greater part of what I am worth," Warren
answered.

Mitchell sank back with a sigh of despair. "I wish
you had talked with me before you became interested
in this wild scheme. But it is too late to say anything
about that now," he said.

Warren took umbrage at once. As a business man,
as a dealer in real estate who was supposed to know
the demands of the market and whose business it was
to anticipate these demands in order that he might
supply them, he was not disposed to tolerate any croak-
ings from a cold-blooded and unsympathetic critic like
his friend ; least of all was he disposed to permit his
sagacity to be attacked in the presence of the ladies,

so he answered almost savagely, "See here, Mitchell, I ought to have known better than to mention any such scheme for the development of the country to any beastly Silurian like yourself. Of course you would cry it down; it's like you and your kind to oppose any step that tends towards progress that we may try to make. You come out here; you get all the advantages of this wonderful climate; you bring your invalids here and get them cured; you eat our fruits, and enjoy our grand scenery, and lead a simply ideal life, revelling in the very poetry of existence so long as you choose to remain; but all this time you keep in mind the fact that you haven't come to stay. You remember very vividly that all your interests are back East; and you are afraid that the truth about this country will get out and hurt your interests as an Eastern man; so you don't see, and won't admit facts as they are; not you! oh, no! You cry the country down because you are afraid the facts will become known; and you say that our development, unprecedented in the history of the world, is all boom, and that it is beginning to collapse already. Oh, I know the whole story you tell; but I think it mighty unfriendly of you to wet blanket me in this manner."

This outburst of virtuous indignation was very fine, and part of it was almost eloquent. It would, however, have made a deeper impression upon Mitchell had Warren been longer than three months in California, and had he not already repeatedly read something of the kind in all the papers issued in Southern California, so that he knew the sad plaint by heart himself. As it was, Warren's impassioned appeal simply disgusted him; and as he paused in his torrent of indignant remonstrance, Mitchell said, "While you are getting your breath, kindly listen to what I have to say. Have I ever misrepresented this country in any way, or tried to detract from any of its charms in the least?—No, don't quibble," he said, as Warren tried to talk around this question. "Give me an honest answer to an honest question. Have I ever, in any way, said less than the truth about this country or its advantages?"

"No," Warren reluctantly admitted, "I cannot say that you yourself have done so; I was speaking of your kind."

"Never mind my kind," Mitchell rejoined. "I want to be egotistical and talk about myself. I have broken the point off your argument; now we will proceed to examine the stump. I believe you say that I accuse you of 'booming;' as I understand that classic phrase, it means creating a market for property in excess of the needs of the country, does it not?"

"I believe so," Warren replied, feeling very cross at being made to appear foolish before the lady of his fond devotion; and as he realized that his want of control over his own temper had drawn Mitchell into this discussion, his anger began to burn hotly against his friend. Of course this was altogether wrong; but, after all, it was human nature.

"Well," Mitchell went on in that calmly logical way which is so convincing but so exasperating, "you are, as I understand your explanation of your idea, creating a suburban town which is to possess all, perhaps more than all, the attractions to be found in any one of the finest suburbs of New York City.

Now, how many inhabitants has Ventura? Three or four thousand, has it not?"

"About that, I believe," Warren replied; his three months' residence in the country having made him so good a Californian that he failed to say about *what*, leaving you to take the larger figures if you chose to do so.

"Very well," Mitchell went on in the same calm, convincing tones, and now prepared to drive his argument so effectually home that it would carry conviction even to so prejudiced and interested a listener as Warren. "New York has considerably more than a million inhabitants, all crowded together on a little island, and this great population must, of course, overflow in one direction or another; that is why all its desirable suburbs succeed. In a town of three or four thousand people, and which has unlimited capacity for extending its suburbs in any direction except, of course, into the ocean, I see no reason for the existence of a suburban town to catch the overflow of population; at least not until it equals New York in population. And I don't expect that even you and your company expect that to come about in less than ten years, do you? There you have the reasons why I say your project cannot succeed. And there, again, you have the reasons why I say that you are trying to create a demand in the market which does not exist in order to supply it with an article no one needs; or, once more speaking in the vernacular, you are 'booming.'"

Warren hastily sprang to his feet and caught up his hat. He was angry with himself for the outburst which had led to this discussion; angry with Mitchell for taking advantage of it to show the rashness of investing so heavily in an enterprise which was at least of doubtful success; while his anger was increased by the fact that he could not answer one of these arguments.

"There is no use of our pursuing this discussion, Mitchell," he answered hotly, endeavoring to control his temper, but with only partial success. "I will only say this in reply to you: 'he laughs best who laughs last,' and in less than a twelvemonth I shall take out at least ten times the money I put into this enterprise, and it is not at all unlikely that I shall make fifteen times my original investment. By that time you will be despising yourself because you were too big a coward to make a dollar, even when the opportunity jumps at you and begs to be taken up. Good-morning. Good-morning, ladies." And, bowing to Mrs. Mitchell and her sister, he left the room.

Mitchell looked after him in silence as he closed the door; then, as he resumed the reading of the morning paper which he had laid aside as Warren entered the room, he said, wiping his glasses as he spoke, "Girls, you have often heard of the California land-craze; you see it in its most malignant form in that young man who has just left the room. Shun the disease,— shun it with the utmost care. It spares neither sex nor condition, while it hardly spares any age; indeed, none are free from the infection save infants and tender youth. Like intemperance and the opium-habit, it carries wretchedness, poverty, and disaster into many a home, and, saddest of all, I fear that its dire work is only just begun. As for that young man, our friend Warren, he is already past cure."

Mrs. Mitchell raised her eyes from the sewing on which she was employed, her alarm visible in every feature. "Oh, John Addison," she cried, "do be serious just one moment, and tell me,—you don't really think he will be ruined?"

"Answering both questions at once, I do," Mitchell replied. "As for being serious, I was never more in earnest in my life than I am at this present moment. I don't like his partner; he is a pleasant and plausible man,—altogether too plausible, and he looks like a sharp. Then, I have seen something of the crowd his business compels him to go in with; I don't like them at all. My opinion is that they have got hold of him for a green Easterner, a 'tenderfoot' as the phrase is, and they won't let him go until they have cleaned him out."

"Oh," Mrs. Mitchell exclaimed, with a sigh, "what a dreadful pity! Can't you do something to help him?"

"What can he do, Effie?" Mollie, who until now had sat silently but intently listening to all that had been said, calmly asked. "You heard John Addison trying to advise Mr. Warren, and you saw how angry he became at any interference, and how he went off in a huff. If he will not take a friend's advice how can any friend help him?"

"That's the point exactly, Mollie," Mitchell answered, resuming his paper. "Nothing can be done. It's the old Scotch proverb fulfilled before our eyes: 'If wilfu' will to water, wilfu' maun drench.'"

CHAPTER VI.

THE fifth of March was a perfect day; the sun rose clear and warm, not a particle of mist was in the atmosphere, while the day itself was as mild as a day in an Eastern June.

By ten o'clock a merry party was gathered under the broad porch of the Anacapa waiting for the horses to be brought round; while a two-horse carriage stood ready for Mitchell to display his skill as a driver.

"Good-by, Effie; I hope no calamity will befall you," Mollie called out to her sister, as Mitchell assisted her into the carriage. She herself was still standing in the door-way of the hotel buttoning the wrist of her long riding-glove.

"I hope that my life will be spared to me; but I confess that I have my fears. The memory of my last ride with John Addison, and how he upset me and hurt my shoulder, still lingers in my mind, calling up awful forebodings as to my fate and the disasters about to befall our heir before we are once more safely back in our rooms," Mrs. Mitchell answered, as she seated herself in the carriage and drew the duster about her.

"If that is his style of driving I think we had better take the lower road; if we go by that, we shall have to cross the creek about fourteen times, and possibly he might upset you in that. The water will break the force of your fall less violently and far more agreeably

than the hard ground," said Warren, who was standing
by Mollie's horse waiting to assist her to mount.

Mrs. Mitchell received this pleasant suggestion with
a cry of dismay. "I'll never consent to go by that
awful road, and if you are thinking of it, I insist upon
getting out of this carriage and going back to my room
this very moment. If we should try to go by that
road we would never get there alive; John Addison
would have us and himself drowned before we had
crossed the creek half of those fourteen times," she protested, pathetically. Then, as another fear suggested
itself to her mind, she asked, trembling with apprehension while she spoke, "Isn't the water awfully high?"

"It is fairly well up," Warren answered, maliciously.
He was still sore over his last interview with Mitchell;
and he was well enough acquainted with feminine
nature, at least in so far as it was displayed in his
friend's wife, to know that if he could thoroughly
awaken her fears before the trip was fairly begun, she
would hold her apprehensions prominently before her
husband not only during the ride to the valley, but she
would also retain enough of them to render him thoroughly miserable during the return journey as well.
This fact brought him a feeling of intense satisfaction;
and, seeing how well he had succeeded in arousing her
apprehensions of the dangers lying before her, he tried
to still further add to them, saying, "Indeed, the last
time I was up that way I found my road cut by a very
respectable stream; but that is all the better for you,
because in case you should really be upset, the deeper
the water and the swifter the current the less will be
your danger of striking the rocks in your fall."

Mrs. Mitchell positively refused to view the matter
in any such comforting light, and would neither be
calmed nor comforted until her husband, thinking that
the matter had already gone too far for his comfort,
interposed. "Don't be a goose, Effie," he said. "We
never entertained the notion of going by the lower road
in the first place; and whichever road we do take, I
will engage to take you up and bring you back safely.
The dangers you will be called upon to encounter are
by no means so great as our friend represents. I see
through his game, and you ought to. He wants to
frighten you, and make you a lively companion for me."

Mrs. Mitchell glanced reproachfully at Warren, who
laughed, raised his hat, and said, "All ready? Drive
on, and we will overtake you by the time you have
reached the avenue."

By this time Mollie had joined him. In her dark
riding-habit and tall hat she looked simply bewitching,
as Warren mentally told himself more than once. Her
soft dark eyes were shining with anticipated pleasure,
while her red lips, just parted, showed the small, white,
even teeth. Warren lifted her into her saddle, and
taking his place beside her, Glenn and Miss Lake now
declaring themselves ready, the party galloped after the
carriage.

For the first few miles little was said between the
riders. Although riding certainly is an exhilarating
and most delightful exercise, it is by no means condu-
cive to sociability; while a young man in love can find
no more exasperating position in which to make the
effort to win the affections of the lady of his choice than
that which he is forced to occupy during a horseback-

ride. Warren was now a sufficiently accomplished equestrian to understand all this; and for some miles conversation was not attempted beyond now and then a few words in reference to the scenery or the route they should follow. Delightful as is the ride to the Ojai under any circumstances, it gained charms far beyond any that Warren had dreamed it could possess from the perfect happiness he felt in the society of his companion. As for Mollie, it would have been difficult for her to define the sentiments which she entertained towards her companion. While she enjoyed his society, yet he awakened in her a strong antagonism, which, perhaps, gave to the man and his opinions an interest she would not otherwise have felt either in reference to Warren himself, his theories, or his conduct. After crossing the creek and riding on at a rapid pace for two or three miles, they drew up under the shade of a grove of live-oaks to rest their horses and enjoy the scenery; while they also waited for their companions, whom they had left at some distance behind them.

"How I wish I had my sketch-book with me!" said Mollie. "I would like to preserve this beautiful place in some more permanent form than my memory; I would like it to refer to myself after I return home, while it is also well worth showing to one's friends."

"While I do not in the least doubt your skill with the pencil, Miss Wade, do you think you could do justice to the scene?" Warren asked.

"Thank you for your implied confidence in my skill, and permit me to congratulate you upon your dexterity in the use of language. No one else among all my acquaintances could so delicately and ingeniously

e

have retracted in the last half of a sentence what he had been saying in the first half as have you only now," Mollie answered, pretending to feel bitterly aggrieved.

Warren raised his hat, saying, "Permit me to most humbly beg your pardon for my stupidity. I am crushed into the earth by the weight of your displeasure; I certainly did not mean to retract anything that I had said."

"Perhaps you will explain your meaning, and in that way permit me to judge your intentions," she replied, without changing from her first injured manner in the least.

"What would I not do to be restored to your favor?" Warren answered, his eyes expressing the earnestness that he dared not permit his words to convey.

In an instant Mollie was on her guard. "Mr. Warren cannot be charged with over-modesty. Why does he think that he can be restored to that which, possibly, he never possessed? But I am waiting for the explanation," she replied.

The words were spoken in the same light and playful manner in which their sparring was habitually conducted; but there was a look in her dark eyes as they met his own which warned Warren that she, like himself, had thrown into her words a meaning she wished him to understand; while he also perceived that if their comradeship were to continue that he must act, for the future, upon this warning she had given him in all his conduct towards her.

Warren flushed and bit his lip. He was hurt more deeply than he would acknowledge even to himself. Still, though it was clear from her words that he had not as yet gained her affections, nor even her liking beyond an indifferent esteem, which permitted her to accept him as an agreeable escort now and then, he would not as yet despair of what might be. Concealing the pain her words had given him as best he might, he answered in a tone as careless as her own,—

"I merely intended to intimate to Miss Wade that she could hardly hope to do justice to the rich coloring of the scenery before us in the colorless reproduction of a pencil sketch."

Mollie glanced keenly at him for an instant; then, seeing that he fully understood her meaning, wishing to place her companion once more at his ease in her society, she dropped her air of pretended indignation, and, as though there had been nothing more in their words than appeared on the surface, she looked long and earnestly at the picture spread before her.

The road wound around the mountains; and just beyond where they had reined in their horses, though concealed from their sight by a turn, it dipped slightly in its descent to the valley below, accomplished by an easy and pleasant grade. On one side of them the mountains rose precipitous and almost awful in their majesty; their wrinkled faces now smiling with the verdure brought out by the winter's rains. A meadow lay gently sloping úp to their sheer ascent, dotted with live-oaks, from whose branches hung long festoons of lace-like Spanish moss; while it was carpeted with bright flowers of all colors, ranging from a dainty and delicate blue to the gorgeous yellow of the California poppy.

On their left was a sheer descent of hundreds of feet

down to the valley below. Through this valley there ran a narrow and shallow river looking like a silver thread in the distance, its banks lined with a green fringe of willows. At their feet, and on into the remoter distance, lay the fertile ranches of prosperous farmers, their green fields looking like huge checkerboards as they extended far up the hills, whose precipitous walls framed the picture beyond; while over all was spread the rich deep-blue canopy of the California sky.

Mollie drew a deep breath expressive of her admiration of the scene before her as she said, speaking as much to herself as to her companion, " No; it would be almost sacrilege to desecrate this beautiful picture with my crude scrawling. Even the most skilful of artists would fail to do full justice to its beauty."

"May I hope, then, that I am justified in your opinion?" Warren asked, wishing to keep up for the present the badinage in which they had been indulging.

"Fully."

"And forgiven?"

"Fully. But what is coming now?" she asked, as the soft tinkling of bells came to their ears, still faint in the distance, but gradually coming nearer.

"No demon of the mountains or the forests. So much the reverse, that you ought to be familiar with the sight by this; it is even so commonplace and homely a thing as a load of wood. Come, let us make room, then wait and see if my prophecy is not fulfilled," Warren answered.

They reined their horses to the side of the road farthest from the precipice, then faced them about, waiting. Again Mollie's eyes wandered to the green fields dotting the distant hill-sides miles away, although every feature of the landscape came out with perfect distinctness in the clear atmosphere.

"What grain is that growing in those fields on the hills over there, Mr. Warren?" she asked.

"Faith, I can't tell you. You could not ask a worse authority than myself as to agricultural matters," he answered, flecking with his riding-whip an acorn from the oak overhanging him as he spoke. "If you were to ask me its value as acreage property you would be within my province, and I would give you an answer in which you would always find my appraisement varying in an ascending or descending scale as you appeared in the character of purchaser or seller. As for what the land produces, there my opinion is worthless. But here comes an authority; let us consult him."

As he spoke the tinkling, which had been continually growing nearer, now sounded close at hand, and around the turn came eight horses, harnessed two and two, drawing, as Warren had prophesied, a huge load of wood piled in three wagons, which were fastened one behind another. The bells were upon the collar of the leader; the driver rode one of the horses next the wagon. When the team had come abreast of them, Warren hailed the driver and put Mollie's question,—

"I say, friend, can you tell us what grain is growing in those fields off on yonder hills?"

The driver reined in his horses, ready to stop for a friendly chat, and answered, "I can that, colonel. That's a mighty fine ranch over there. Yer kin raise anything under the sun and moon over there. See them white spots off on the hill over thataway, lookiu' like a graveyard ? Them's hives. That's a bee-ranch ; and there's a right smart o' bees over thar, yieldin' a right smart o' honey too. They gave suthin' over a ton last year. Then, off on the hill that away,that green field's barley. Then, off thataway, that smaller field's spuds."

Mollie looked sadly perplexed as this unfamiliar name was spoken, thinking at first that she had misunderstood. Glancing from Warren's amused face to the bland and serious countenance of the driver, she said, " I beg your pardon ; but I don't think I understood that last name."   -

" I say, them's spuds," he explained, as he discharged a huge quid of tobacco preparatory to refreshing himself with a fresh chew.

Mollie's face became almost pathetic in her perplexity.

" I—I fear I don't *quite* know what that is. Does it grow out of California ?" she asked.

" It grows the world over, Miss Wade," Warren answered, laughing heartily at her puzzled expression. " One does not often hear the word in household life, even in this part of the world, where I believe it is alone indigenous. But 'spud' is the commercial name in California for the potato."

" O-h-h !" said Mollie, prolonging the interjection ; and, touching her horse with her whip, she dashed down the road unceremoniously, and was around the turn and out of sight in an instant. Bidding the friendly driver "good-morning," Warren galloped after her, and soon overtook her—indeed he found her waiting for him—in an oak grove at the foot of the hill.

Checking his horse at her side, Warren asked her, as soon as laughter would permit him to speak, "Why did you take your departure so very unceremoniously, Miss Wade?"

"I hope you did not think that I was running away from you, Mr. Warren," Mollie answered. "I assure you that I had no such intention. But while I am willing to do *almost* anything for your sake, I cannot— I *cannot*, even to enjoy the delights of your society, remain in the presence of a man so wholly lost to the better instincts of human nature that he can call that useful article, the potato, by such a horrible name as 'spud.'"

Warren placed his hand upon his heart and bowed low in his saddle. "For myself, thanks awfully. For your explanation, it is sufficient, and I share in your sentiments fully. Yes, in every particular," he added, hastily forestalling the question he saw her about to put. "I altogether agree with you as to the charms of my society, while I share your feelings of horror as to the name of the vegetable we have just heard. But look," he said, pointing up the hill. "There come our dilatory companions; shall we wait, or ride on before them?"

"Let us wait," she requested, anxious to avoid any further attempt at love-making.

Warren, of course, assented; so, waiting until the rest of the party were close upon them, they then turned their horses and rode on, still keeping sufficiently in advance to be by themselves.

"Mr. Glenn does not seem to be an accomplished horseman," Mollie remarked, glancing back towards the other pair of equestrians in the party as she spoke.

"No," Warren answered, also looking back to observe them. "He seems to be almost as much of a tyro as Miss Lake. In her case her want of skill is pardonable, for she is an Eastern girl. In his case there is no excuse, for he has been out here for years, and every Californian rides."

"As they have safely come so far on their journey, I suppose we need not feel anxious about them?" Mollie laughingly asked.

"Not at all. Their riding is safe even if it is not beautiful," Warren answered, in the same spirit as that in which the question had been asked.

"Be careful of your criticisms, sir; I am an Eastern girl as well as Miss Lake," Mollie severely returned.

"But you know how to ride," Warren protested.

"Oh, yes," she answered, "I have always known how to ride. I have spent half my life at least in the country and so among horses, and I cannot remember a time when I did not know how to ride. But most of our Eastern girls are not so fortunate as to enjoy such opportunities for learning the art of riding as have always been mine. But how far are we from our destination?"

"A little more than two miles. Are you tired?"

"Tired? No indeed! I could ride forever in this delightful air and warm sunlight."

A brisk ride of a few minutes over a road as hard and even as a floor and the party were in the street of a quiet village nestling between two spurs of the Sierra Madre Mountains, the high peaks towering up towards the blue heavens on either side. The street was shaded by huge live-oaks, while green fields lay on either hand.

"What a lovely place!" Mollie exclaimed, her eyes sparkling with delight and admiration.

"Is it not?" Warren asked in reply. "To my mind this is the veritable Happy Valley. It is rightly named Ojai, is it not?"

"I am afraid I am not qualified to pronounce judgment on that point," Mollie answered. "I did not know, until this moment, that the word possessed any meaning."

"The natives tell us that it does," Warren returned. "Tradition says that it is an Indian word meaning 'Eagle's Nest;' and, to my mind, no more beautiful or appropriate name could have been given to this lovely valley than that by which its savage possessors first called it."

"It does perfectly describe it," Mollie answered. "It does resemble a huge nest held in the arms of the mountains."

"There is our destination," said Warren, pointing as he spoke towards a group of pretty cottages whose white sides gleamed out in pleasant contrast to the green of the oak-trees beneath which they nestled. "It is a unique way of building a hotel, is it not?" he added. "This grouping together a little village of neat cottages. But I like the idea; it harmonizes so perfectly with this delicious climate and romantic country."

"Yes," Mollie answered, "and the name is appropriate and self-suggestive in this instance also. As one looks at these great trees gracefully draped in moss, which shade the buildings, the name 'Oak Glen' comes to one's lips almost of itself."

Assisting her to dismount, they stood waiting upon the veranda of the principal cottage until the rest of the party came up; then Warren said, as the others dismounted and came up to where he and Mollie stood waiting,—

"Now what is the verdict? Shall we have dinner now, or shall we wait and rest? Don't all speak at once, please. Mrs. Conyngham, what do you say?" turning to the Rector's wife, whom Mitchell had that moment handed from the carriage.

"I am not at all tired, while I am very hungry," that lady replied.

"I think we all share the same sentiments," said Mrs. Mitchell. "A grace of fifteen minutes will be sufficient for us to repair the damages incurred during our journey."

The merry party was soon gathered around the table in the pleasant dining-room of the Oak Glen cottages.

"I rejoice to see that you have safely encountered the manifold dangers of field, forest, mountain, and flood," Warren said, addressing Mrs. Mitchell in a manner as serious, and conveying as much congratulation, as though she had safely come through the most deadly perils.

"You may laugh at me all you choose, Mr. Warren, but I assure you it is no small tax on one's nerves to ford streams, and ride up mountains and through passes, behind two spirited horses which are managed by an unskilful driver," she answered, severely.

"Only hear that now!" her husband interposed, twisting his face into what he intended should represent the keenest mental anguish. "And that from my own wife! You would think that the horses had been managing me, instead of I them. But the proverb is true, and I see it substantiated in my own family every day: no man is great to the members of his own household. I must remember that I do not suffer this misery alone."

"You did very well indeed this time, John Addison," his wife answered, in a tone at once conciliatory and patronizing. "You did not commit one reckless act, and you were not *very* awkward. But you cannot expect me to place implicit confidence in your driving after you have once upset me."

"That was more than three years ago, and I hear of it every day of my life; and I suppose that I shall until my life is ended," said Mitchell, laying down his knife and fork and looking around upon the members of the party, every feature of his countenance making a pathetic appeal for their sympathy.

"I think it very likely that he may have upset you purposely, to give you reason for the want of confidence in his skill which you were expressing at that very time," said the Rector, addressing Mrs. Mitchell.

"Thank you, thank you, Mr. Conyngham," Mitchell answered, his manner expressing the consolation these words afforded him. "That is a suggestion I shall always highly value. My dear, will you kindly bear in mind after this, that I capsized you through skilful driving, and not out of awkwardness? and tremble in silence for the future lest a worse fate befall you."

"Warren! do take your fingers out of your mouth!" Mrs. Mitchell's voice rang out sharply above the merry conversation of the little party. The whole company started in surprise, the mild-mannered little Rector dropping his eye-glasses into his plate in his consternation, while Mr. Glenn turned and stared at his partner, wondering if his hostess had taken sudden leave of her senses that she should think he could be guilty of such a breach of good manners. For a moment all eyes were fixed upon Warren, who was quietly eating his soup when Mrs. Mitchell spoke. He started so suddenly at her sharp voice that he dropped his spoon to the floor in his confusion ; then, turning several colors at once, he stooped to pick it up.

As soon as the words had left her lips Mrs. Mitchell remembered how they must sound to her companions, and covering her face with her hands she cried,—

"Oh, Mr. Warren, forgive me ! I spoke to my son, not to you. But I cannot say any more ; words will not help matters at all."

Warren glanced across the table at Mollie ; and, as their eyes met, she burst into a merry laugh, in which he joined, amused at the absurdity of the situation in spite of his sudden start and confusion.

"I cannot say that I should heartily enjoy such an occurrence at a state dinner-party ; but in an informal gathering where we are all so well acquainted I think I shall survive it ; only please don't repeat the experiment too often," Warren said in answer to Mrs. Mitchell's explanation.

"My dear, your power over me is forever broken," Mitchell gravely remarked to his wife. "Never in my worst moments did I make such a break as that. I shall, hereafter, use this little affair as a counter-irritant."

His wife looked up at him beseechingly, but made no answer.

After dinner the party broke up; the men going off for a walk, and to enjoy their cigars: all, that is, save Mr. Conyngham, who, as he did not smoke, remained with the ladies to escort them around the village. After supper Warren invited Mollie to accompany him in a moonlight ramble.

She threw a lace wrap mantilla-wise about her head and shoulders, and they strolled together through the quiet village street.

"I am more than grateful to you for suggesting this excursion, Mr. Warren. But for you I should never have come here; and I should have gone home without visiting one of the prettiest places in the country," she said, looking up into the brilliant starlit sky as she spoke.

"I fear that Mitchell would never have undertaken the journey without the strong persuasion we employed. There are disadvantages as well as advantages attaching to his size, are there not?" Warren answered.

Mollie laughed as she replied,—

"In his profession he is industry personified; but he does bitterly hate anything like physical exertion."

"Now, my own case is just the reverse," said Warren. "I never yet shrank from any amount of fatigue which was undergone in the pursuit of pleasure; while the very thought of *work* would invariably do me up completely. I did not know that I could work six months ago. Were you ever in Italy?"

Mollie looked at him, surprised at his abrupt change of subject.

"No. Why?" she answered.

"The question was not prompted by any profound ideas struggling for expression; I hope you do not think it, for if so you are doomed to disappointment. I was merely thinking, when I spoke, of what we so continually hear and read about, the beautiful Italian skies; and I was wondering if they could surpass the skies of California," Warren replied.

"I cannot picture to myself a sky more lovely than this," she said in her soft, musical voice, again looking up with dreamy eyes to the brilliant stars. "Its warmth and brightness are the very pledge of health and life."

Warren looked at the fair face, so sweet and pure in expression, and never more fair than now, bathed in the soft moonlight.

"Yes," he answered, "it is a feeble illustration of what a pure love can make the life of man. It transforms and beautifies him; and its magical influence makes him as unlike what he once was as this fortunate country, blessed by its genial atmosphere, is unlike the frozen East."

Mollie looked quickly at him, half startled, half amused; then she dropped her eyes as she answered, "I did not know that you were a poet, Mr. Warren."

"Nor am I, unless being inspired by one's own experience be to possess poetic gifts," he replied, looking at her so significantly that she could neither evade nor ignore his meaning.

"I am not an unbeliever in the power of love," she answered, her lips trembling as she spoke. "How can I be, when I daily see so many lives made happy by it? But, after all, I think that friendship is to many a safer and a better guide through life. Love, sometimes, is only a bitter-sweet; friendship has all the sweet and none of the bitter; all of the sweetness that can ever exist in love comes from the element of friendship which must always enter into it. So, in friendship, one has all the gain with no possibility of the loss love must sooner or later bring to those who accept it."

Warren listened to her words sick at heart. He understood her delicate reproof of his attempted courtship now as thoroughly as he had done in the morning. He had intended to test her; he wished, so far as might be possible, to make sure of her sentiments towards himself before risking his present, possibly his future, hopes upon the chances of an open declaration. She had understood his purpose; and, unwilling to give him needless pain; unwilling to end the good-fellowship existing between them; wishing to spare him the mortification of appearing before *his* friends, *her* sister and brother, in the guise of a rejected lover, which the termination of their companionship would reveal even though the secret were preserved by them, she at once seized upon the opportunity that his words afforded her of delicately warning him that she was in earnest in desiring him to look upon her as a friend, and to attempt to gain no closer intimacy.

"Friendship," said Warren, bitterly, unable to wholly conceal how deeply he was hurt. "Yes, when this is offered one who wishes more, it is like the offer we are told of, where one offers a stone to him who asks for bread."

Mollie returned no answer, but silently walked at his side, still looking down upon the ground. Warren's arm trembled under the light touch of her little hand resting upon it; and, after a moment's silence, she raised her eyes to his, saying,—

"Come, it is late; we ought to return to the cottage."

Without making any reply he turned back with her. Silently they walked to the cottage side by side, and simply bidding one another "good-night," they parted until the morning.

Until the morning! To Warren it seemed as though death itself could not have parted them more widely, more cruelly, than those few words spoken during that short walk. They would meet, it was true, when the sun brought in another day; but for him the meeting would have more of pain than of pleasure. The stronger grew the hunger of his longing, the farther some unseen, intangible, perverse influence was drawing them apart.

f

CHAPTER VII.

When Warren returned to Ventura he found that, in addition to his own sorrows, he was likewise fated to aid others in bearing their griefs.

The Elkins household was in confusion. There was nothing at all worthy of especial note in this fact when it was considered by itself; for it was seldom, very seldom, that tranquillity reigned over this domestic realm with peaceful and undisputed sway.

Warren had accurately described his landlady when he called her a "California Yankee." Mrs. Elkins was fifty, and perhaps a little past this age. She was tall, and as straight as that mathematically accurate tree, so wearisome and exasperating in its correct proportions, the Norfolk Island pine, a specimen of which adorned her own gardens; while she was *almost* as slender, and *almost* as unbending in her nature. Her features were sharp; her eyes were shrewd and piercing; her lips were thin and closely shut.

She had never known an hour's sickness in her life, and was unrelenting in her contempt for those less favored than herself in this respect. In her disposition she was what the natives call "a hustler." She had no idea of the meaning of tranquillity herself, and she permitted no one else to enjoy it, so far as her power extended to end its dominion. Although, at her husband's death, he had left her almost wealthy, she had never permitted this fact to soften her life in the least;

f

but she worked as hard, lived as frugally, and saved as carefully as in the days of poverty which she had known in her early married life. Although she was a woman of strong affections, and was devotedly attached both to her husband and her son, it would have seemed to her the merest weakness to manifest any outward signs of affection ; and while inwardly she had adored her husband and mourned his loss every hour of her life, and little less than idolized her son, outwardly she was as hard as iron, sarcastic and fault-finding, and was as consistently merciless to him as to herself. Industrious to a fault, from early morning until far into the evening she was overburdened with work ; and, although she was up before the sun, like the English statesman immortalized by his over-activity, she "seemed to lose an hour out of the beginning of each day, and lived in a whirl, vainly trying to catch up."

Knowing as well as he did by this time the character of his landlady, it would have caused Warren the greatest surprise to find the house in anything less than a turmoil ; but he at once saw that the present tempest was of extraordinary severity, and that it had its origin in causes of greater consequence than those which usually prevailed.

"Well, well, Mrs. Elkins, what is the matter? Jake, are you in disgrace again?" he asked, as he came into the dining-room, where Jake was sitting the picture of despair, while his mother was whirling about, a perfect cyclone of combined wrath and industry, trying to sweep and to scold at the same time.

"Yes, it is Jake," she cried, angrily flourishing her broom. "I have as good a mind to break this over his head as ever I had to do anything in my life."

"What has he been up to now? Put down your broom and let me hear about this fresh calamity," said Warren, seating himself on the lounge as he spoke, and laying his hat and overcoat by his side.

"You may try to laugh it off, Mr. Warren," Mrs. Elkins answered, with fire in her eyes, "but it's no laughing matter, I assure you. Here's Jake, spite of all I could say or do, 'd keep hanging around a nasty Greaser girl; and last night that old Greaser, her father, drove him off, like he'd been a dog. That was bad enough, even if a white man 'd done it. But that my son—a decent boy, and the son of a respectable man—should be hounded round by a dirty, low-lived Greaser: it's more than flesh and blood can stand." And Mrs. Elkins began sweeping furiously, in the vain attempt to work off her wrath.

"See here, mother," Jake said, firmly, and looking more manly than Warren had ever seen him appear before. "Don't talk like that about Camilla: it seems like I can't stand it to hear you. You may say what you like about me, and I don't mind how much you cuss the old man, but you mustn't run down Camilla. She ain't no Greaser, and you know it. She's a nice girl, and you know that too. I ain't goin' to hear nobody say no bad things about her, not even you."

"Are you going to turn against your own mother, Jake?" Mrs. Elkins asked, with her tears lying very near the surface.

"No! I ain't goin' to turn against nobody. I know what I owe you; I know what I owe her; and you

ought to know what you owe the girl I'm goin' to
marry. All I ask is that you'll treat her and speak
of her as you ought," Jake answered.

As soon as she heard this challenge to her hitherto
unresisted authority the tears were all gone and the
fire once more blazed in Mrs. Elkins's eyes. "You
marry her, indeed! I think I see you doing it!" she
exclaimed, with the bitterest scorn in her voice. "Before you can marry her you've got to get her out of
that house first, and into this house over me next; and
what I want to know is, how you're going to work to
do it?" And once more the broom was called into
active service.

Warren was anxious to get at the merits of the case
and cure the difficulty, if there were any cure for it;
but to do this he must first stop Mrs. Elkins's flow of
bitter words, which would not be possible while the
irritating cause continued in her presence. Her power
of caustic eloquence was, unfortunately, almost unlimited, and she always gave full play to her feelings.
Nothing remained, therefore, but to get Jake by himself and learn the whole story, and then see what could
be done for him.

He was the more anxious to do this because he
saw that, underneath the lad's uncouth exterior, there
was a fund of good principle and a wealth of good
material which only needed to be brought to the surface to make of him a manly and a valuable man.
Unfortunately, he had never had any proper home-
training, and he was in great danger of becoming
utterly idle and shiftless for that reason; but, with a
motive before him, and with a fair chance in his start

in life, he was equally likely to come out all right. The motive, Warren felt sure, now existed in Jake's true affection for his Spanish girl; the chance he was anxious to make for him, and he thought that he would soon have an opportunity of doing this; therefore he was anxious to keep good his present influence over him. So, rising from his chair, he said,—

"Jake, I have a little work I would like you to do for me this morning; come down to the office."

Jake rose listlessly from his chair, as though life possessed no further charms for him and it made no manner of difference where he went or what he did.

"Now, Jake," his mother exclaimed, "don't you go where you hain't no business to be, and get in trouble and bring worse disgrace on us than you have already."

"Don't worry Jake or fret yourself, Mrs. Elkins," Warren answered. "I will see that he is all right; I shall not lead him very far astray."

"Oh, I know he's all right so long as he stays with you, but he won't keep with you all the time; then, when he gets off by himself, there's no telling where he'll be or what he'll do." And with this parting shaft she banged the dining-room door after them as they passed out into the hall and then to the street.

Jake's was not a strong character, certainly. He was not manly; he was not self-assertive; while he was altogether too ready to submit his judgment to the opinion of others, and to yield himself to another's guidance, with the inevitable result that he was universally regarded by all who knew him best as a great, good-natured, lubberly fellow who did not amount to very much and never would.

8

Warren, however, looked beneath the surface. He perfectly understood the fact that it would require more moral strength than usually falls to the lot of man to stand against Mrs. Elkins's masterful nature; while, for a son trained from his earliest years to hear and obey, this would be little less than impossible. It had become a second nature to Jake to yield to his mother's will and implicitly obey her wishes, and this he would continue to do so long as he continued to live with her and remain dependent upon her. That there was good stuff in the young fellow Warren was certain; and all that was wanted to bring him out, and transform him from an overgrown boy into a man, was to get him released from his mother's overwhelming influence.

"I have my carriage all ready for us, you see. I am going out into the country a short distance to look at some property, and I want you to go with me," Warren said, as they reached the sidewalk.

"All right, sir; I don't know of anything to prevent; seems like I'd as lief do that as anything else," Jake answered, as he climbed into the carriage.

As Warren took the reins into his hands he said, "Now, Jake, you don't seem very chipper this morning. I want you to tell me all about your trouble; and remember that I meant what I said when I told you that I stood ready to help you in any possible way."

"Thank you, sir," Jake answered, despondently. "I don't think you can do much for me. I think of goin' East, though. If you know anybody back there who'll give me a job I'll be glad of that."

"Going East!" Warren exclaimed, in surprise. "What on earth is taking you East?"

"You see it's this way," Jake answered, resolved to make a clean breast of the matter, sure, at least, of obtaining sympathy, even if Warren should prove to be unable to render more substantial aid. "Last night I met Camilla at the house of a friend of hers, and when she was ready to go home, of course I went home with her."

"Of course," Warren answered; "and I suppose it is equally of course that you went to that friend's house without the slightest notion that the young lady would be there. These chance meetings are always purely accidental."

Jake grinned feebly, but made no other answer; then resumed once more the thread of his story of painful adventure.

"After we got to her house we stood in the yard talkin', when out come the old man, madder 'n a hatter, and sent her in. Then he took me by the collar and told me that he'd known what was goin' on a good while, and had been layin' for me. He was goin' to put an end to this now, and if I ever dared come hangin' round there again he'd shoot me; then he run me off the place. I could 'a' busted him easy as nothin'," Jake added, clinching his huge fist as he spoke, "and I come mighty near doin' it once; but I remembered he was Camilla's father and an old man, and so I didn't. Now that darned brother of hers 'll go and tell about it all over town, and it seems like I couldn't stand it, so I guess I'll go East."

Warren felt his respect profoundly increased for the

young giant at his side, who had submitted to indignity rather than put forth his strength against an old man, and the father of the girl he loved, even though he knew at the time that he was subjecting himself to the charge of cowardice and want of spirit, and exposing himself to the ridicule of his friends.

"You did right, Jake, very right," Warren said, cordially commending his conduct. "You have shown yourself a brave man. It would have been no act of valor on your part to use your strength against an old man, while it was a brave thing in you to keep your temper and restrain yourself under strong provocation. It is always cowardly to do wrong, and it is brave to do right; while it is the braver thing to do the harder you find it to do."

Jake looked comforted. "I was kind of afraid to tell you, because I thought you'd think I sneaked off like a whipped cur," he answered.

"Not a bit of it," Warren cordially replied.

Oftentimes the least promising scions, by virtue of careful pruning and cultivation, become the finest and most profitable trees in the orchard. Perhaps this tribulation through which Jake was now passing was the very pruning process necessary to bring out the best that was in him. Warren felt convinced of this in his own mind, and he resolved that it should be through his counsel, advice, and assistance that his faculties were put forth in the right direction. The feeling that he was being of real use to some one, and that he was doing something to promote the fortunes of another, was a novel sensation to Warren, whose career had been, up to this time, the idle routine of pleasure characteristic of the young man of wealth. He found it a pleasant experience, however, and the *rôle* of " My Lord Bountiful" was one he thoroughly enjoyed, not only because it ministered to his self-importance, but also because it strengthened his self-respect. The idle life he had hitherto lived had not been chosen of deliberate intention. Like other men, he had accepted the career which had been opened before him by circumstances and the accident of birth as the one which he ought to accept without question. He had floated with the tide, not because this course best pleased him, but because he knew of nothing else to do. The pleasure to be derived from lending a helping hand to one who needed his aid came to him like a revelation, and, as he always entered into everything that he attempted with all his heart and soul, he determined to do everything in his power to assist his *protégé* in the advancement of his fortunes, while he was equally desirous of obtaining all the pleasure possible for himself in doing it.

"You say you are going East, Jake. Have you made up your mind where you want to go?" Warren asked, flicking a fly, which was displaying remarkable adhesive qualities, from his horse with the lash of his whip as he spoke. The spirited animal, accepting this as a hint that those behind him were anxious that he should do better in his time, jumped violently ; then, setting back his ears, whirled over the road at almost double his former speed.

"Careful, Mr. Warren ; this ain't no horse to monkey with, and this ain't just the place to show tricks in drivin'. There's a turn in the road ahead of us, and I'd rather take time goin' down into the valley," Jake remonstrated. Then he added, in answer to the question Warren had put to him,—

"No, I hain't no choice where I go; I don't know nobody out of Californy, so it can't make no manner of odds to me where I fetch up. All I want is to get out of this; and I was thinking of Denver, or perhaps Salt Lake."

Warren had not, as yet, become altogether accustomed to the Californian's habit of speaking of everything on the other side of the Sierra Nevadas as "East;" therefore, as he still regarded these two cities, like every other Easterner, as being in the remote West and located on the very confines of civilization, Jake's locating them in the "East" seemed to him delightfully absurd, and he laughed heartily; then, observing Jake's look of hurt surprise at a merriment which seemed to him altogether uncalled for, Warren controlled his amusement and answered,—

"I'll tell you frankly what I think, Jake: my opinion is that you had better stay right here. You have not given up your young lady because of last night's misfortunes, have you?"

"What do you take me for, Mr. Warren?" Jake indignantly answered. "She ain't to blame for what happened. Of course I sha'n't give her up. I'm goin' to stick to her through thick and thin, and she's goin' to stick to me."

"Then what do you want to go away for?" Warren urged.

Jake looked steadily at the horse's tail, as though the caudal appendage of the animal before him had suddenly developed some new and hitherto undiscovered interest for him.

"Well," he answered, "I thought it would be pleasant to get away from home for a while and see the world."

Warren looked his companion fully in the face as he said,—

"To tell the truth and shame the party whom truth is popularly supposed to put to the blush, you want to get away so as to dodge the talk. Isn't that about plumb centre of the target?"

Jake fidgeted a little, then answered, desperately,—

"You've hit it, Mr. Warren."

"Now, Jake," Warren went on, in the friendly, persuasive tone which never failed to carry conviction to the soul of an unwilling investor, and which invariably brought him up to the purchasing-point,—"Now, Jake, you don't want to spoil the whole business by flinching at the last moment. I advise you to stay here and go to work. It won't be fair to Miss Carballo to go away and leave her to face the talk alone,—in case there is any, which is by no means an established fact,—and it won't be fair to yourself. You know the old saying about the unfailing tribulation which belongs to every love-affair ; and you can't expect to be an exception to the general rule. There are by far more hopeless cases than yours."

This last Warren said in a sad tone, as he thought of his own difficulties.

"What kind of work had I better do?" Jake asked.

"I will find something for you, if you will only agree to do it," Warren answered.

"I certainly will," Jake replied, with a ready acquiescence which Warren had by no means expected.

"That, I think, is your best plan," Warren continued. "If you can make a home for yourself and wife, that will put an end to all the present trouble. You are of age, and so is the young lady. There may be opposition on the part of your respective families,—indeed, we know that there will be,—but time will settle all that; so, if you will do as I say, your case is very far from hopeless."

"I'll stay here and work like—like a man," Jake answered, speaking more cheerfully than he had done before during the ride.

They had now reached the property Warren had come to inspect. It was late in the evening before they turned towards home; and after arriving in Ventura, as they parted at the stable, Jake to go home, Warren to go to the hotel for his supper, he sadly thought upon his *protégé's* courtship, and contrasted it with his own. In Jake's case, a happy issue seemed almost certain to come about sooner or later; for himself, he dared not hope for such a result. Opposition from without was not the most fatal enemy to happiness, even though this was manifested by the parents of those chiefly concerned. With him, the contest was against the young lady's own indifference to himself. Were Mollie even averse to him, he would regard his prospects as being far more hopeful, for even this would show that she did sometimes think of him, at least often enough to discover reasons for disliking him. But as she could not be brought to think of him at all, there was clearly nothing before him but a life-long heart-hunger, destined never to be appeased.

CHAPTER VIII.

"This letter is from Tom." The information was given by Mrs. Mitchell, who was seated in the large bay-window which formed the corner of her sitting-room; a pleasant seat, and one which not only gave her the full enjoyment of both mountain and ocean scenery, but also commanded a prospect far up and down the main street of the town, permitting her to observe all that was going on, while it also afforded her the privilege, so dear to the feminine heart, of seeing how the female portion of humanity which thronged the sidewalk below was attired; of commenting on the taste, or want of it, which was there displayed; and of remarking to whomsoever might, at the time, be in her company, that one of the passers-by was becomingly arrayed, while the taste of another was wretchedly bad: "She simply has *no* idea at all how to dress, my dear; only look! her clothes couldn't look worse if they had been thrown at her." But Mrs. Mitchell's thoughts were otherwise occupied this afternoon, for the Eastern mail had just come in, and she had been made happy with a large packet of letters from home. Tom, in whose epistle she was now deeply absorbed, was her brother, many years older than herself, a prosperous business man, and happy in the possession of a large family, a proportionately larger fortune; and happiest of all, the politicians would have told him, by his residence in that great

93

State among whose citizens he had the honor of being enrolled,—Ohio.

"This letter is from Tom," Mrs. Mitchell again remarked, without raising her eyes from its pages.

"Ah !" Mitchell, replied, without raising his eyes from the important business letter he was engaged in writing, in answer to one he had just received, and with his mind so wholly occupied with the work in hand that he had not heard a word of what his wife had been saying.

"Yes," she answered, reading from the letter in her hand ; "he says that his oldest girl has been very sick indeed."

Mitchell's thoughts were far away ; indeed, they were at that moment on the Atlantic coast with the troublesome client whose letter he was then answering. Although he had heard nothing, like a dutiful husband he felt called upon to make some kind of an answer ; so, without raising his eyes, or suspending the rapid scratching of his pen for a moment, he replied at random,—

"That's good, I am sure."

"Good !" Mrs. Mitchell indignantly exclaimed, looking up from her letter with a glance of withering scorn. "Would you think it '*good*' if our little Warren were to almost die of pneumonia? You have not been paying the slightest attention to me, and you have not heard a single word of what I have been saying."

"My dear," Mitchell replied, with his customary serenity of manner, "consider me humbled to the earth by your scorn, but let justice be tempered with mercy, and remember that I have a very important business matter in hand; and, being only a man, I have not your feminine capacity for doing several things at once and doing them all equally well."

Mrs. Mitchell laughed, but her retort was checked by the entrance of Mollie, who, at this moment, came into the room dressed in her riding-habit, but looking tired and very much out of temper. Laying her hat on the table, she dropped upon the lounge with a profound sigh, and began to draw off her gloves.

"Did you and Mr. Warren have a pleasant ride, dear?" asked Mrs. Mitchell, at the same time handing to her sister the letter she had already read.

"Oh, yes, the ride was pleasant enough, I suppose," she answered, indifferently.

"What is the matter, then? You look thoroughly out of sorts," Mrs. Mitchell persisted.

"I am; I feel literally and completely exhausted by the mechanical pursuits in which I have been engaged," Mollie replied, leaning back on the lounge and clasping her hands behind her head.

"Mechanical pursuits?" repeated Mrs. Mitchell, throwing several interrogation points into her tone and looking completely mystified; while Mitchell, who had not followed the conversation, but had overheard the last remark, held his pen suspended in the air on its way to the inkstand, looking at her in surprise.

"Yes," she answered; "so I think I may call it, since I have been busy for two mortal hours rigging a guy."

"See here, Mollie," Mitchell interposed, deeply offended at Mollie's slighting reference to her late escort; and, throwing down his pen as he spoke, he rose from

his chair, his voice and manner expressive of more
anger than he usually permitted himself to display,
and which he himself afterwards said he thought "un-
becoming in a man of his weight in the community,"
—"see here, Mollie, I cannot permit you to use such
language in reference to any gentleman whom I admit
into intimacy with myself and family, and whom you
receive as an escort yourself. How do you justify any
such epithet as applied to Mr. Warren? You know
yourself that he is an accomplished gentleman."

" As far as clothing is concerned, and when manners
are also taken into account, I admit he is a gentleman.
But, apart from these, I find very little in the young
man to challenge admiration," Mollie replied, not in
the least dismayed by her brother-in-law's indignation.

"I would not admit the fact, Miss Wade; the confession speaks very little for your good sense or your
character. Do principles have no weight in your estimation of a man? or have you not brains enough to
appreciate education when you meet it?"

Mollie still remained uncrushed, and answered with
that same air of utter weariness with which she had
entered the room,—

"To use your own words, which you are so very
fond of repeating, 'a man's merits depend more
upon the use which he makes of his acquirements than
upon what he possesses;' and as, so far as I can see,
Mr. Warren makes no use of his education and very
little of his principles, on the basis of your own wise
maxim, he might almost as well be without them."

This was even worse than calling him a mental and
moral guy; and, as her charges were altogether un-

founded, and as Warren was no more deserving of the bad opinion she now expressed of him than he was of her scorn, Mitchell determined to adopt a course which, as it happened, was the only wise one for him to pursue, that of making her define her accusations and defend her charges. In this way, and in this way only, would it be possible to bring her to reason and make her retract her words.

"You have made a very sweeping statement, young lady," he answered, sternly, to her last caustic speech. "Now you must maintain your position by giving me positive proof of the truth of your words, or else I shall insist upon your apologizing for such language. What do you mean by charging my friend with want of principle? You must remember that such a charge reflects upon me as well as upon him, and it amounts to accusing me of admitting a scoundrel into intimacy with my family."

This was severe upon Mollie, for she had not had any definite idea of her own meaning when she spoke, and had merely uttered the words in a pique growing out of a momentary misunderstanding with Warren, without thinking how her words would sound to others, while they conveyed no real meaning to her own mind. She was, however, too thoroughly a woman to be left without a reply; so she answered, with the same indifferent tone and manner in which she had spoken ever since she entered the room,—

"You read in my words a meaning that I certainly had no intention of conveying. All I meant was, that it certainly takes no great amount of education to delude poor unsophisticated Easterners into speculating in real

E   g   9

estate; and after sitting so long as I have beneath the droppings of your wisdom, I have had it strongly impressed upon my mind that this is not a calling calculated to produce the highest mental or moral growth."

In spite of his anger, Mitchell could hardly keep himself from smiling at the girl's determination to defend herself by quoting words she had heard him speak from time to time in reference to the prevailing rage for speculation; while he felt his indignation gradually disappear as it became clear to him that her severe words were really without meaning, and were promoted by no deeper feeling than a passing pettishness growing out of some recent disagreement with his friend. He abated nothing from the severity of his manner, however, and answered, as gravely as before,—

"Mollie, my only regret that Mr. Warren is engaged in his present calling is based upon the fact that I fear he may do himself a serious injury; I know him well enough to be sure that he will not, intentionally, injure others. He will do his best to make every Easterner realize a handsome return from his investments; and remember that a man can be just as honest in real-estate operations as in any other calling. I also think that it would be well for you to remember that words are dangerous things, and that you should use them with corresponding carefulness. And I must say, Mollie, that if you dislike Mr. Warren so cordially, it is in very bad taste for you to be so much in his company."

"Who says that I dislike him? I am very sure that I never said so," Mollie answered, with true feminine inconsequence, rising from her seat as she spoke, and gathering together her belongings, together with the letter which her sister had given her, preparatory to going to her own room.

Mitchell seated himself at the table again with a sigh, and took up his pen with an air of utter hopelessness.

"Well, Mollie," he said, "being a woman, you are, of course, incorrigible; and, like every other woman, you can reason only in a circle. I judged of your sentiments towards Warren merely from your own words, and they certainly indicated that you felt anything rather than friendly towards him."

Mollie went to the door, partly opened it, then stood hesitating a moment with her hand upon the knob before she answered,—

"To be sure we are friends, and I suppose that is the reason we don't like each other any better. We are bidden to love our enemies, you know, but nothing is said about *friends;* and I am afraid that I am not a good enough Christian to think very highly of my friends, even if it were commanded; they let me know them altogether too well for that."

As she closed the door, after delivering this parting speech, Mrs. Mitchell, who had been silently listening to the conversation, looked up with a glance of shrewd intelligence and said,—

"John Addison, if that is not for all the world like a man!"

"What peculiarly masculine proclivity have you recently added to the already long list of discoveries which has rewarded your painstaking researches into my character?" Mitchell asked in reply to his wife's exclamation, dipping his pen into the ink as he spoke, and preparing to once more resume his interrupted letter. Without directly replying to this question, Mrs. Mitchell came over to where he was sitting, and, seating herself by his side, laid her hand upon his, with a gesture half caressing and half coaxing, while she looked up into his face with an expression in her eyes that he by no means understood.

"Well, my dear, what is it? Why does black care sit like a brooding shadow upon your usually smiling face?" he asked.

"John," she began, very seriously,—"John, answer me truly. Would you be very sorry if Mr. Warren and our Mollie were to become fond of one another?"

Mitchell once more laid down his pen, wondering in his soul *when* this letter would ever be finished; and, leaning back in his chair, he took his wife's hand affectionately in his own and, patting it caressingly, replied,—

"Why, no, certainly not! She could not have a better husband than he would make her; while as for Mollie, a man might go the world over without finding so nice a girl as she, now that *you* are out of the case. But what put that idea into your head? I see no signs of an ardent and increasing affection between them."

Mrs. Mitchell shook her pretty head with impressive seriousness and demurely answered,—

"No, John, I did not suppose that you would have noticed anything; you are only a man, you know. To a woman's keen perceptions the signs are very clear indeed; and now I want you to understand me, John," she added, with playful severity: "I am no match-maker, and for all the world I would not make or mar in the matter, yet I would not be sorry to see it come about, and I asked your views in reference to the situation because you are doing everything in your power to break up any liking for the man that Mollie may already have growing in her heart."

This last she said while tapping his hand with her fingers to give emphasis to her words. Mitchell was completely taken aback by this charge; he could hardly have been more overcome had his wife deliberately charged him with being the chief promoter of the Sharon case, or laid to his account almost any other affair, past or present, of which he knew nothing and in which he felt very little interest.

"Why, goodness gracious, Effie!" he exclaimed. "What do you mean? This affair is none of my business, and I hope you don't mean to accuse me of meddling in love-matters. What have I done?"

His wife laughed merrily at his consternation and disgust, and at once proceeded to enlighten him as to his sins, though at first rather vaguely, saying,—

"I can think of very little that is stupid that you have not done, while you seem to have a perverse inspiration which prompts you to keep on in your ridiculous proceedings."

Mitchell's round, good-natured face now became overcast with a very serious expression.

"Please explain yourself, Effie, and let me definitely know my sins," he replied.

His wife at once complied with his request and proceeded to unfold before him the long catalogue of his offendings.

"To begin at the beginning," she said, "you know that Mollie and Mr. Warren first met under very embarrassing and, to her, distressing circumstances. You, in your idiotic love of a 'joke,' were the one who brought about this painful situation by needlessly bringing them face to face, and then, as I have always thought, very meanly leaving them to extricate themselves as best they could from the difficulties in which that unhappy exchange of trunks had placed them. Of course the whole situation was absurd, but you made it painful, which it had no need to have been. While Mollie is sufficiently fair-minded not to let all this prejudice her against the man, she would have to be either more or less than human if it did not create in her mind an antagonism towards him ; and this you have all along taken the utmost pains to increase by doing as you have done to-day, for instance,—I mean, by arguing with her about every little pettish speech to which she gives utterance, which really means nothing at all, and is prompted by nothing deeper than mere girlish pique."

Mitchell sat fairly aghast and wholly defenceless as his wife poured the overwhelming volume of these charges upon him.

"Do you mean, Effie, that I ought to permit her to make any absurd accusations against Warren the whim of the moment may dictate, and do nothing to make her see her injustice?" he asked, after a moment's silence necessary for collecting the ideas Effie had put to utter rout.

"I mean that I look deeper than you, my dear," she replied, "and I see underneath this manner which is so distressing to you a growing liking for Mr. Warren and for his society. She herself is half conscious of this, and the old antagonism, which is your own work, remember, causes her to criticise him and find fault with his doings. Now, Mr. Warren is no nearer perfect than any other man, and is, consequently, open to criticism. If you say nothing and pay no attention to her little bitter speeches beyond laughingly checking her when she is unreasonable, the matter will take care of itself. But if you make a serious thing of it, you will waken all the antagonism she has ever felt into opposition to yourself and hostility to him, and she will end in simply hating the man."

Mitchell did not know what answer to make to this. He was not versed either in the history of love or in the laws by which it works; neither did he understand the principles which underlie that most mysterious of all things, the workings of a woman's mind; so he sat listening to his wife with a feeling of utter helplessness, which manifested itself in his inconsequent answer,—

"I am no match-maker, Effie; that is not a man's business. I prefer not to interfere."

Again Mrs. Mitchell's laugh rang out merrily. "That is exactly what I have been asking all this time," she answered. "I don't want you to interfere; and what I am asking is, that you will simply let the child alone. Don't magnify every little manifestation of pique into a serious matter; be patient even if she is foolish and unjust; remember that she is really vexed with herself, not with him; and, while she is seemingly blaming Mr. Warren, the truth is that she is scolding herself for liking the very man whom she thinks herself almost in honor bound to dislike."

Mitchell was about to reply, but his answer was cut short by a knock at the door; and, rising from her seat, Mrs. Mitchell opened it to usher in the person under discussion. He greeted them with a cordial "Good-evening, friends," as he entered the room, at the same time placing on the table a large package which he had been carrying.

Mitchell thought within himself, as he welcomed his friend, that, however troubled the course of love might be in his case, he certainly gave no external evidence of distress, but carried every outward indication of being a prosperous and happy man to whom the world was giving all that he could reasonably ask. But this was the masculine and unreflecting manner of looking at the case. Had he spoken of his thoughts to his wife, or had he even taken counsel of his own pride, either one of these monitors would have told him that, of all disappointments, this was the very one which must be carefully concealed from the world. However confiding a man may be by nature, however freely he may display his sorrows before his sympathetic friends, he cannot go about like the Mater Dolorosa in the religious pictures, with his transfixed heart held prominently before the gaze of all beholders; but, however cruel his pain may be, with Spartan courage he must conceal his sufferings behind a smiling countenance.

"Good-evening," Mitchell replied, returning his friend's greeting. "You fulfil the old proverb, for we were discussing you just as you came in."

"Indeed," Warren answered, seating himself and beginning to undo the package as it lay on the table

before him. "In what way have I verified the wisdom
of our ancestors, by the rustling of wings, or by the
display of a cloven hoof?"

"We regard you as possessing wings, of course, Mr.
Warren ; it is needless to ask us our opinion of you,"
Mrs. Mitchell replied.

"Thanks, awfully !" Warren answered. "Consider
me with my hand upon my heart bowing low before
you in graceful acknowledgment of your pretty speech.
My hands are too full of these documents, however, to
permit my making any physical response."

"What have you got there?" Mitchell asked, rising
and coming to Warren's side in order to see for himself.

"I have come to explain that very point," Warren
answered. "These are the bills advertising our great
Oakdale land sale which comes off next Monday. You
have, none of you, ever seen a true California 'boom ;'
and although I know, of course, that you will not invest, yet I want you all to go, for such a sale as this
will be is one of the sights of the age."

"Ah !" Mitchell observed, as he read over the prospectus Warren gave to him, "this is the culmination
of the scheme that you were mentioning to me some
few weeks back, is it not?"

"Yes," Warren replied. "Things are now ripe for
a 'boom,' and we are going to have a big one."

"You go the full figure, I see."

"Yes ; extra trains, free lunch, brass band, and all,"
Warren answered, laughing.

"We must certainly go, John Addison," Mrs.
Mitchell interposed. "It is unlike anything that we
ever have at home, and if we do not see it we shall

lose one of the most interesting sights our country can show us."

"No tourist has fulfilled the true purpose of his pilgrimage unless he has taken in a 'boom' auction sale; and it not infrequently happens that he is taken in at one. Of course we must go; but we must carefully guard against the last terrible possibility," Mitchell answered. "What's your hurry? Sit down," he added, as Warren, having again tied up his package, rose from his chair and prepared to go.

"I can't stay; I have a good deal to accomplish between now and Monday," Warren replied.

"Sit down, Mr. Warren; it certainly will not take you long to stop just a minute," Mrs. Mitchell urged.

"Thank you; but I must not remain even that brief length of time. I have to see that these bills gain an extended circulation. I will call again, though, before Monday," Warren answered, and, bidding his friends good-by, he took his leave.

CHAPTER IX.

THE Monday made memorable in the history of Ventura City and County by being the day of the great Oakdale land sale dawned fair and clear. It is hardly necessary to say this, for weather never enters into the calculations of a Californian. The rains were now over until the following winter; there was no fear of either clouds or showers to mar the pleasure and ruin the temper and the clothing of the participants in any outdoor enterprise. Fog, however, was a possibility, though the probabilities were that, should any appear, it would all blow away before mid-day. But even this slight annoyance was wanting, and the day dawned with nothing to dampen the enthusiasm of possible purchasers, or to ruffle their tempers. If climate and weather combined could make the Oakdale "boom" a success, nature certainly was smiling upon it, and the great land sale, so far as she could further its interests, would long be remembered as among the greatest and most brilliant successes of that land of great enterprises successfully projected, Southern California.

From early dawn the streets of Ventura had been thronged. Horsemen in picturesque variety of costume and mounted on every description of the genus horse, from the sober and sedate animal born of many generations of careful and trusty family servants to the fiery-eyed, half-wild bronco, were galloping to the scene of the sale. The sidewalks were thronged with pedestrians drawn from all sorts and conditions of men : swarthy Mexicans and fair Anglo-Saxons; sunburned ranchmen and well-kept, carefully-dressed tourists; here and there a face darker than the others told the spectator that its possessor was one of the very few now to be found endowed with a strain of the old Indian blood ; while mingled with the rest could be seen the bland, smiling, but withal shrewd face of John China- man, watching with keenest interest these latest pro- ceedings of the " Mellican man."

About half-past eight o'clock the sound of music was heard far down the street, sounding loud and clear above the hum of voices and the sound of the city streets. A brass band, seated in a band-wagon which was decorated with flags and covered with bills and flyers advertising the sale, drove slowly through the streets on its way to the scene of the auction, followed by a long procession of carriages which continually received new accessions.

The crowd thronging the street and sidewalks now began to lessen rapidly, as the throngs made their way in 'buses, express-wagons, or on foot towards the station, where a special train was waiting to take all- comers to the now vacant tract, soon (if the visions of the projectors of the scheme became realized) to be covered with the beautiful villas, elegant homes, the substantial business houses, not to mention the grand churches and unrivalled school buildings of that pros- perous, growing, and beautiful city, Oakdale, which, although it was counted as a suburb of San Buenaven- tura, was destined to become a rival to the metropolis of the Santa Clara Valley of the South herself; while in beauty, in healthfulness of location, for picturesqueness of scenery, for softness and evenness of climate, she would be equalled by few and surpassed by none of the cities of the known world.

So the projectors of this grand enterprise talked; so their advertisements read; so some of them honestly believed.

The climate of Southern California is unsurpassed by any in the world, while that of the two sister counties of Ventura and Santa Barbara has been pronounced by competent authorities, whose judgment may be received with implicit confidence, to be, in many ways, even superior to that of the world-famed Riviera. Since this southern country had, as was universally conceded, a brilliant future before it, why should not this new city of Oakdale, in a very few years, rival either Nice or Mentone?

It never dawned upon even the shrewdest, keenest, and most far-sighted of these speculators, in the excitement of his real-estate frenzy, to stop long enough to ascertain if there was any reason that a city *should* grow up where they had located this new town site; it had never dawned upon the sharpest of them all to look deep enough into the matter to see that the interests of commerce and the trend of population gave every reason why a town should not grow up there, at least for many long years to come.

The shrill whistle of an incoming train told the listening crowds that the "Special" from San Francisco and Los Angeles had now arrived, thronged with passengers who had taken advantage of the less than half rates offered them to come down for an excursion and see the sights, while the Oakdale speculators, who had chartered the train, devoutly hoped that they would all invest.

As the train whistled into the station, Warren crossed Main Street towards the corner of Palm, making his way to the Anacapa. He found Mollie in the ladies' waiting-room endeavoring to read the morning paper, but too profoundly interested in the crowds coming and going through the street to maintain any sustained interest either in the "local" or the "telegraphic" columns. She rose as Warren entered the door of the hotel, and, laying aside her paper, stood waiting for him, welcoming him as he came towards her with a cordial and friendly smile.

"We must be on our way at once, Miss Wade; the sale begins at ten o'clock, and it is already past nine," Warren said, as he waited to escort her to her horse.

"I have been ready for some time. I am not the delinquent; and for once in your life you cannot say, 'These women! they are forever behind time!' I have been waiting for you ever since Mr. and Mrs. Mitchell went to the train, and that is a good half-hour," Mollie answered, as he assisted her to mount.

"I acquit you of all blame; I am the culprit, but I assure you that I am an innocent one. Those maps must be got off, and I had it to do. As I was going to ride and could not take them, I had to carry them to the train, find a trustworthy messenger, and despatch them by him, and all this took time and delayed me," Warren answered, taking his place at her side.

Side by side they went down the street on a smart

trot, not breaking their pace as they went up a short rise, then out into the open country.

"Do you know," Mollie said, as they lessened their speed sufficiently to make conversation possible,—"do you know that in many ways you remind me of my brother Tom?"

"As the gentleman you have named is so near a kinsman of your own, I should, other things permitting me, take this speech as conveying the highest compliment you could pay me. But, judging from the tone of your voice and the expression of your face, I feel a haunting dread that you do not mean it as such, and I am burdened with a distressing apprehension that he is far from an amiable person," Warren replied.

"Oh, you are altogether wrong," Mollie hastily rejoined. "Tom is one of the best and loveliest men that ever lived ; but he is always making appointments at which he is invariably late, and then he is in a terrible hurry to make up the lost time."

"Your experience leads you to think that this is the most strongly-marked trait in my character?" Warren asked.

"I would not say that, but I think it is a very striking trait ; I cannot remember that you were ever yet on time at any appointment you have made with me," she replied.

"This is a very serious charge, Miss Mollie," Warren answered, pretending to look very grave. "I am sorry, deeply and truly sorry, for the inconvenience I have caused you by always being a little behind time, and then hurrying you in order to make amends for my own unpunctuality."

"Oh, I did not say that, either," Mollie answered, blushing slightly at his wilful misinterpretation of her words. "I did not say at all that you resemble my brother in that; on the contrary, you always seem to have time enough and to spare, no matter how late you may be. Until this morning I never knew you to say that you could be a loser on account of lost time."

"I act on a principle laid down by my old rector at home," Warren replied, as he reined his horse closer to that of his companion. "I remember on one occasion, while he was waiting for the arrival of certain parties who were to meet him at an appointment to which I had accompanied him, after a half-hour had passed by, and still there were no signs of their coming, he turned to me, saying, ' I have made one serious mistake in my life by always being punctual. The amount of time I have thrown away during my lifetime by always making it a point to be punctual myself is simply appalling. Had I my life to live over again, this is the first of my great mistakes that I would rectify.' "

Mollie laughed heartily at this frank confession of delinquency as a moral principle.

"So you are trying to avoid the good rector's fatal error?" she asked.

"That is my idea," Warren answered.

"Do you think it a good business maxim?"

"Certainly; just think of the facts for a minute. By being from five to ten minutes late every day I save, taking the lowest estimate for a basis of calculation, at least half an hour every week. Now take that saving for fifty-two weeks, even if we reckon my time as worth no more than a day laborer's, you see I make a handsome percentage for myself every year, and one well worth looking after."

Again Mollie's merry laugh rang out, the sweetest of music to Warren's ear.

"That way of looking upon unpunctuality and reducing it to an exact science is novel to me, I confess," she replied. "I will recommend it to Tom, and perhaps he will be wise enough to profit by your suggestion and turn what I have always before looked upon as a serious vice into one of the brightest of virtues."

They had now come to a point where the road turned off, winding back among the hills into a quiet sheltered nook formed by a bend in the mountain range. On one side lay the ocean, its waters sparkling like crystals in the sunlight; on the other were the hills, stretching away to the Sierra Madre Mountains, whose peaks towered up against the blue line of the sky in the remoter distance. Towards this pretty nook the vast concourse of people, coming by different roads, was gathering as a common centre, while distant scarcely more than a quarter of a mile below stood the train from Ventura and the "Special," each discharging its passengers, who were wending their way up the slope to this same point.

"There is our destination," said Warren. "Let us tie our horses here and wait for Mitchell and your sister; they will be up here in a few moments now."

Dismounting himself and assisting Mollie to alight, he fastened their horses to a live-oak, while they meantime stood waiting for their friends to join them, silently drinking in the beautiful scenery the while. Mollie found enough to interest her, for the scene was a novel one to her Eastern ideas.

The Oakdale tract, comprising several hundred acres, had been surveyed and laid out into streets and avenues crossing each other at right angles, and dividing the town site into blocks of equal size, while each block, in its turn, had been subdivided into lots. At the intersection of these streets were posts bearing the name of each intersecting street, while smaller posts, each bearing a letter and a number, marked the boundary of each lot.

Near the centre of the town site was a large depression of nearly an acre in extent, called in the California terminology a "dry lake." This, during the rains, received the drainage of the surrounding hills and was filled with water, but during the long rainless summer it was wholly dry. Already the water was almost gone from it, and its bed was fast becoming transformed into a marshy pool overgrown with rushes and rank grass.

Beyond this dry lake rose a low round hill, standing isolated and alone between the lake-bed and the foot-hills, its summit crowned with a thick growth of oaks, while the whole town site was laid out in a dense grove of oak-trees which had only been partially cleared away, and which covered the sides of the hills and the cosey nook nestling between them, making the name Oakdale at once appropriate and suggestive.

In the centre of the town site and on the margin of the dry lake a stand had been erected covered with a canopy of red-white-and-blue cloth, and decorated with flags ; while its framework was wholly concealed with bunting. On this stand was a table the top of which was covered with maps; behind it the auctioneer was sitting, while back of him benches were placed, on which the band was seated vigorously playing patriotic airs.

Underneath the oak-trees, and at some distance from the band, were tables laden with meats and fruits, the lunch provided by the Oakdale company for all who attended the sale.

Mollie was profoundly interested, almost absorbed, by the lively picture presented in this, to her, unusual sight. Every class of men and women was represented, from the keen-eyed, sharp-faced speculator, watching for a good investment, to the tourists, attracted by the novelty of the scene. Here, the representative of some rival land company, with sneering face, was walking arm in arm with some would-be investor, to whom he was pointing out industriously the wild folly of trying to plant a town in such a location, and proving to him that in its very arrangements the evidence of bad faith on the part of its projectors could · be clearly seen by any one who would only take the trouble to look carefully into the matter. There, the inevitable tramp was sitting under the trees near the tables, hungrily waiting for the call to lunch, and perfectly willing to take his land wherever he might find it, and his climate by the wholesale under porches and sheds, and in open box-cars; while walking around under the trees were many young couples with no thought at all beyond a holiday passed in the society of one another.

"What do you think of the scene?" Warren asked,

studying intently the varying expressions passing over Mollie's bright face.

"It is profoundly interesting," she answered. "It is a scene of even absorbing interest to me, for I have never seen anything at all like it before. It seems to me, though, to be more like a public celebration than like an auction sale."

Warren smiled as he answered,—

"I never thought of that before, and I don't know but that is the way in which we ought to regard the sale. A land auction means the building up of this finest section of the country, does it not? so, by a happy inspiration, we have introduced the band and the free lunch, and have by an opportune blunder brought in features which have a propriety in themselves."

"Yes," Mollie returned, in the quaint tone peculiar to her, which always amused Warren while it also produced in him the uneasy feeling that he was being laughed at; "the California land sales combine the essential elements of a picnic, Thanksgiving, and the Fourth of July."

"They are something after that order," he answered, and then added, "Here come our friends! Let us go and meet them, and then I will explain a few of the ideas of our company before the sale begins."

"Gracious, I'm dead beat out! Why did you not put your town a little nearer to the railroad, or else bring the railroad a trifle nearer to your town?" Mitchell gasped, as he came puffing up the slope and threw himself down under the shade of the nearest oak.

"If you will observe, you will see that the road up which you have just come is a broad avenue, running through the town from the railroad station on its south side to its northern limit; this avenue will be bordered with palms and magnolias, and a cable road will run through it," Warren answered.

"Well," Mitchell retorted, "it's ten thousand pities that the cable road was not built before the boom struck you. I never was so blown in my life."

"Everything in due season. Are you too tired to listen to our plans? I have ten minutes in which to explain our ideas to you before the sale is called," Warren answered.

"Go on; I'm all ears," was Mitchell's reply.

"Yes, that's a family characteristic, I believe," Warren answered; then, without waiting for his friend to recover sufficient breath to return a Roland for his Oliver, he began his explanations.

"You notice the dry lake and the little round hill just beyond it? We propose to reserve these with sufficient land around them to make a handsome park. The hill we shall clear off and build a reservoir upon its summit, bringing the water from some streams a number of miles back in the mountains. Then we shall terrace the side of the hill towards the lake, and coat these terraces with bituminous rock; then we shall turn the water down this terraced fall into the lake, keeping it always full and also making a picturesque cascade. We shall stock the lake with fish, and we shall also import swans and put them upon it. The hill itself will also be handsomely laid out, while we propose to place around the reservoir some specimens of as handsome statuary as can be found anywhere in the State. The streets around the park, or circles, as you will notice that we call them, are to be reserved for residences which are not to cost less than a certain specified sum."

"That's a grand idea, and it will make one of the finest towns to be found anywhere in the world, if you can carry the scheme through ; but have you counted the cost?" Mitchell replied.

Warren cast upon his sceptical friend a glance of the intensest disgust as he answered,—

"Of course we have. I can assure you, for your comfort, that we shall have more than enough money to successfully complete all that we have planned after this sale is over and our ideas have become widely and thoroughly known."

Further conversation, either in the way of explanation or of discussion, was now prevented by the auctioneer, who glanced at his watch, rose from his chair, and, pounding with his mallet on the table before him, began his opening address in the following words :

"Ladies and gents, it gives me the greatest pleasure to see so goodly an attendance at this sale, and I am especially pleased to learn that so many of you are strangers.

"California is, at last, becoming known. People are at last waking up to the fact that there is a part of these great United States where snow never is seen, off the tops of the highest mountains ; where frost is unknown ; where the tenderest flowers are always in blossom in the open air, and where strawberries ripen in the gardens twelve months in every year. The Easterners are now just beginning to realize all this, and to find out that by coming here they can get away from their snow-drifts and blizzards, and find a spot where they can, for once in their lives, get thoroughly thawed out. Farmers, also, are finding out that instead of working in a barren rock-patch from four o'clock in the morning until sunset, then lighting up their lanterns to go out and finish their day's work by lamp-light, and working like this from youth to hoary age in order to get enough together to die in the poorhouse, they are beginning to wake up to the fact that they can come here and find rich soil, take life easy, and let kind Mother Nature do their farming, while they get rich in the operation.

"Now, it is this general waking up to the fact that a new Garden of Eden exists right here, in Southern California, that makes such projects as this sale of to-day necessary. It has taken the East a long time to wake up. Their long, hard winters make them sleepy, just as it does their bears and their woodchucks; but now that they have begun to open their eyes, they are coming out here with a rush, and they pick up our new towns faster than we can lay them out.

"And of all the new towns that it has ever been my happy fortune to place before the public, it has never been my lot to offer any in so fine a location, with so equable a climate, and with so well-projected a survey, as you now see in this lovely nook which I am offering to you this morning, known as the new city of Oakdale."

He then proceeded to describe the ideas of the company as Warren had already explained them to his friends, and then closed his harangue by stating the terms of the sale, which were the customary one-third cash before sunset, one-third in nine months, and the balance in one year, at ten per cent.

Maps were then distributed to all who were present at the sale, showing the town site with its division into streets and town lots; and as each block on the map was lettered, while each lot was numbered, corresponding to the letters and numbers on the posts, a glance at the map gave each person an accurate idea of the plan of the projected town, making it possible for those desiring to purchase to choose with perfect accuracy the sites and locations which seemed to them the most eligible; while to further aid investors in reaching a decision as to where they would prefer to place their investments, a man bearing a flag upon a pole went from street to street, stationing himself upon each lot as it was put up for sale, making it possible for the bidders to see exactly how it lay in its exposure, the scenery it commanded in its outlook, and also—and this is an important item in estimating the value of land where the difference between sunlight and shade is so strongly marked as it is in the semi-tropical climate of Southern California—whether or not it was so situated that it would receive a fair amount of sunshine.

The preliminaries being now all arranged, the auctioneer issued a command to the standard-bearer of the sale, who forthwith moved off in obedience to orders, and placed himself on the lot to be first offered to bidders.

The auctioneer at once called for bids, crying at the top of very powerful lungs,—

"Now, ladies and gentlemen, I offer to you, as you see, Lot No. 1, in Block A, of the town of Oakdale, county of Ventura, State of California. This is only another way of telling you that I am offering you a lot in a town situated in the finest county of the West and the grandest State in the Union. Where can you find such another climate as we are blessed with in all the world? Where can you show me so fertile a soil as that of this Santa Clara Valley of the South? You have all of you been spending the winter in California, and you know for yourselves that I am telling you the plain, unvarnished truth, and that I don't say anything but hard, solid facts. In all the world you can't find such another country as this. No colds, no coughs, no consumption, no hay-fevers, no catarrhs, no malaria. Why, bless you, these facts do all the talking for themselves; I don't need to say anything, and I ain't a-going to. Now, I stand here offering you all a chance to own a home in this vale of Paradise, where you can sling a hammock under your own vine and fig-tree, and swing in its easy embrace all the year round; while you can gaze off over the limpid waters of the Pacific, sparkling like diamonds in the sunlight, your brows fanned the while by the soft ocean-breezes, or kissed by the gentle zephyrs from the mountains, whose sweet breath comes to you laden with the perfume of myriads of flowers.

"Now think this over, and tell me, in your bids, what you offer for this first lot ever put on sale in this new town, which I predict will, inside of ten years, rival Nice or Mentone in the Old World; tell me what this prospect of peace, health, wealth, and happiness is worth to you."

The auctioneer paused to catch his breath and waited

for the first bid, eagerly scanning the faces before him, his own countenance alert with shrewd humor.

The agent of the rival company was standing directly in front of him, his face twisted into an expression of the deepest scorn, both for the auctioneer's eloquence, for the town site, and for the whole proceedings.

The bid was not forthcoming, and the auctioneer again found it necessary to add an incentive to the zeal of those before him.

"What am I offered for this lot, located, as your own eyes tell you, on the Pacific Circle, right across Pacific Avenue, the main avenue where the cable cars will run, and facing the Park? No house can ever be put up in front of you; your outlook will always be upon one of the prettiest parks any city in the country can boast of; while over and above all this, you have an unobstructed view out over the ocean. Now, what do you offer me for this lot, one hundred by two hundred and fifty feet, remember?"

"Two dollars and six bits!" The bid was made by the agent of the rival company, and he threw into the tones in which he made it all the bitterness of his soul. Every one in his vicinity turned and looked at him in blank amazement; while those who were out of his immediate neighborhood stood on tiptoe, craning their necks in order to see who it was who had made so unprecedented a bid.

The auctioneer at first started back in surprise; then, thinking that he might have misunderstood the offer, he said, "I beg your pardon, sir; what was your bid?"

"I said two dollars and six·bits, and I stand by it.

As an investment the lot is worthless; but I think the wood on it may be worth the money," snarled the rival of the Oakdale Land and Water Company.

Glenn, who, like Chaucer's Reeve, was a "slender, choleric man," started forward, burning with fury, intending to inflict some serious bodily injury upon this base-spirited emissary who had come up, like Satan in the mediæval legends, from some dry and desert spot to work mischief in this fair garden of beauty. Warren was, fortunately, standing close beside him, and, placing his hand upon his partner's arm, he urged him to be silent and control himself, for the auctioneer was a man whom they could safely trust to bring ridicule upon the enemy; and this was the only weapon with which they could hope to defeat him and save themselves from the ruinous loss which now threatened them.

Glenn clinched his fists and stood stamping his foot in impotent fury. If this malicious bid should create suspicion of bad faith on the part of the company and stampede the possible purchasers, all the expenses which the company had incurred up to this time would prove money thrown away, while the expenses of to-day's sale would also be additional loss. Disaster stared them, one and all, in the face; but a fist-fight would not mend matters in the least. Glenn himself saw that there was nothing for it but patience; so, with grated teeth and clinched fists, he stood glaring with angry eyes upon the calm, sneering face of his rival.

A California land auctioneer is a man of ready wit and brazen assurance, while he is also fertile in expedients; it is at any time hard to catch him unprepared with an answer, and this man was worthy of all Warren's confidence in him.   Seeing the state of the case at a glance; and seeing, also, from the countenances before him that all his eloquence, past as well as to come, was hopelessly thrown away if he could not create a diversion in his own favor, he replied, without an instant's hesitation,—

"Thank you, thank you, sir! Ladies and gentlemen, you see standing here before you a poor, forlorn, broken-winded, shattered wreck from Kansas. I can tell that he comes here from Kansas by his thin, gaunt form, his haggard features, and his pinched nose. Half starved from living on a soil that can produce nothing better than rattlesnakes, his health broken down by blizzards, and his bank account busted by bad crops in the off years and grasshoppers in the on ones, he has wandered over here to buy a home and mend his fortunes. He says that he's only got two dollars and six bits left, all that his folly in not coming to California in the first place has spared him out of a handsome fortune. He offers it all—all he has got in the world—for a home in Southern California. Don't outbid him! Don't, I beg of you, ladies and gentlemen! And I declare this lot sold, as an act of charity, to our bankrupt, broken-winded, deplorable friend from Kansas, and take my word for it, sir, you won't have to wait long for mended fortunes. What name, please?"

The listeners roared, even the irate Glenn suffered his features to relax into a frosty smile, while the disconcerted emissary of a subtile foe slunk back out of sight, lost himself in the crowd, and was seen no more.

"Ah !" the auctioneer exclaimed, "our deplorable friend tells me that on searching his pockets he cannot make good his bid and he asks the privilege of forfeiting his purchase. So I declare that sale off, and again call for your bids.

"What am I offered for this lot, big enough for you to put a mansion on it, and then have grounds enough left for a stable in the rear and handsome lawns? What am I offered? Start it, some one !"

After some spirited bidding the lot was knocked down for five hundred dollars, and the standard-bearer was sent to a lot on the slope of the hills, on the other side of the auctioneer's stand.

Again he called for bids.

"Here you have a lot, not quite so large as the last, but a good-sized lot, though, one hundred by one hundred and sixty feet, on the corner of Santa Clara and Ramona Streets, southern exposure, and having the glare of the sun tempered by pepper- and erysipelas-trees already set out by the company. What am I offered ?"

It is to be supposed that by the last-named botanical marvel he referred to some small eucalyptus-trees which the company had recently planted; but as he did not further explain his meaning, no one ever certainly knew.

This lot started very well,—one hundred and seventy-five dollars were immediately offered. This was at once raised to one hundred and eighty dollars by another bidder; who, in his turn, was also outbid by five dollars.

The auctioneer was delighted. "That's it, gentlemen," he cried, striking his hands together. "Now you've got hold of the idea of how these sales ought to be conducted. It's going to just boom here by and by. Eighty-five—eighty-five—eighty-five—eighty-five I'm offered.—Ninety—will—you—make—it? Eighty-five—eighty-five—eighty-five—who'll—go—the—ninety?"

Looking at a group of men standing in front of him and a little apart by themselves, busily talking together, he called out, "Here, you fellows over there, don't talk to one another; talk to me. Just tip me a wink; I can hear that ten blocks off. Eighty-five—eighty-five—eighty-five.—Ninety—will—you—have—it? Thank you," in reply to a bid to that amount.

"Now, see here! Here you stand like a group of graven images, and you are letting lots be bid off for one hundred and ninety dollars that you'll pay one thousand dollars for, and think that you've got 'em cheap at that figure, in six months from now, after the station is built and the population comes streaming in here in great volumes, like the falls of the Yosemite when the snow is melting on the mountains.

"Going at ninety—at ninety—at ninety—at ninety—at ninety.—Ninety-five—will—you—make—it? I'm looking right straight at you fellows over there, and some of you are going to get killed when this bargain goes off and hits you."

After some further spirited bidding, which, however, did not get out of small figures, the lot was knocked down to a graceful, handsomely-dressed woman for three hundred and thirty-five dollars,—a woman who, already possessed of wealth and of high social standing, like many another of the fair sex in California, was afflicted with the land-craze in as acute a form as any real-estate agent in the country.

The man with the flag was now .sent to wave his standard in a street a little to one side of what was marked on the map as intended to be the business section of the town, and the auctioneer began his address by an explanation, which he made in the following words :

"Ladies and gentlemen, I am now offering you a lot which I do not think is a very desirable one. The Oakdale Company proposes to put up on the lot right across the street from this, which they have reserved, . a school-house to cost thirty-five thousand dollars. Although the lot is only three and a half blocks from Pacific Avenue and the cable road, this lot is too near the school-house for me, and I wouldn't have it. I'm an old bachelor, though, so I suppose you ladies think my opinion ain't worth much, and I suppose you're right ; and you married men who have walked the floor night after night with crying babies also look at the matter in a different light from what I do ; so, what'll you give me to start this lot right across the street from the new thirty-five-thousand-dollar-school-house ? You start it at some figure : you young man with a straw hat and blond moustache, I mean. Give us a bid, won't you ?"

The designated individual blushed modestly, looked sheepish, and offered seventy-five dollars.

"I am offered seventy-five dollars for a lot seventy-five by one hundred ! One dollar a front foot I am offered for this lot !" the auctioneer cried, throwing the deepest scorn into his tones.

"That young man is also a bachelor, that's very evident. Will some married man raise?"

After a pause, and a moment of deep silence: "Will anybody raise him?"

Another pause; still silence reigned.

"Isn't there even one married man in all this crowd?"

Another pause, during which the modest young bidder drew back in the hope of concealing his burning blushes in the crowd. The auctioneer leaned over, scanning the faces before him, and cried,—

"Isn't there a married woman here to raise that bid?"

Again he paused, then cried, with a face expressing the intensest anxiety,—

"Haven't we got a parson here who will marry off some of these people so that we can find somebody to sell this lot opposite the school-house to?"

A snicker went the rounds of the crowd, and a voice from the outskirts offered one hundred dollars for the lot.

"Ah!" the auctioneer exclaimed, heaving a sigh of profound relief, while his face showed that once more life possessed charms for him. "The fire has broken out in another part of the city; now you'll see business done! One hundred dollars I am offered for this lot in the fashionable quarter of this city; one hundred and one, will you make it? Why, bless your dear hearts and stupid heads, this land is rising in value every minute while you stand there cogitating whether or not you dare invest. Don't stand staring one another in the face! Walk right up here and make your offers like little gentlemen! The ladies, too, bless your pretty faces! We want you all here. We want you for citizens. One hundred I am offered for this choice lot. Will any one give me one hundred and ten? No? Say nine, then.

"No? Well, we'll call it eight.

"No? Then say seven.

"No? Well, we'll jump down to three. Who'll give me three?

"No one? Well, one, then. Will that bring you to time? What's the matter with this town, anyway?"

He now stopped in his flow of talk, and, looking round upon the faces before him, he broke out in a voice trembling with emotion, and speaking in tones which told the assembled listeners that the tears lay very near the surface:

"Can't I get one bid? Not even one? Isn't there a single man or woman in all this throng who will give me one dollar, just one little dollar, when it will save the homestead, the dear old homestead, where the date- and the fan-palms wave their graceful foliage in the perfumed breezes; where the roses blossom all the year in the open air; where we have played together in childhood's happy hours through the long sunny days, and been so happy,—oh, so happy! Can it be that I am offered not one paltry dollar, when it will save the dear old homestead?"

Then, suddenly changing from the pathetic, he began, in mildly persuasive tones, to argue the point.

"Why, friends," he said, "just think of the fabulous prices these lots, now going begging, are going to bring inside of five—no, inside of three years. You don't seem to realize how Jonah's gourd grows out here. What was Pasadena ten years ago? Where were Riverside and Orange then?

" I am coming closer home, and ask you about how much Ventura, over there, amounted to only ten years ago ?

"So I could stand here all day and tell you about big cities and thriving towns here in Southern California, that eight and ten years ago men would hardly take a lot in as a gift. *Now* you can't touch one in any of them unless you cover it all over with coined gold, and fresh from the mint at that.

" Why, bless your innocent hearts, what are you afraid of here ? Anything is perfectly safe in Southern California. We are selling lots to-day for hundreds that you'll have to give thousands for inside of a twelvemonth, if you let them fall into the hands of speculators."

Just whose hands they were in now he did not see fit to explain.

After some urging the lot was finally sold ; and, as it was now noon, the sale was adjourned until two o'clock, and the company was invited to lunch.

The band struck up a waltz, and the whole thronging attendance—investors, speculators, and spectators—made their way to the tables, where a bountiful lunch was provided at the expense of the Oakdale Company, and of which all were welcome to eat as freely and as much as they chose.

Warren lunched in company with his friends, and as he helped Miss Wade and her sister he asked,—

" How do you like it as far as you've got ?"

" It is as good as a play ; I never saw a more amusing creature than that auctioneer. What a Koko he would have made !" Mollie exclaimed, laughing heartily at the recollection of his droll expressions and queer grimaces.

"Yes," Mitchell dryly remarked, "when this little bubble has burst the world will be the gainer; that is, if he will only go on to the metropolitan stage."

Warren looked deeply injured.

"What do you mean by that, Mitchell?" he asked, almost angrily. "Did you not hear what he said about towns that ten years ago were, some of them, not in existence, and that now are large, thriving, growing cities?"

"Certainly," Mitchell answered, not in the least overcome by this argument. "He might have said, though he did not, that ten years ago Los Angeles did not amount to much, while to-day it is a great city whose brilliant future I dare not attempt to predict."

"Then what is the matter with Oakdale?" Warren asked, indignantly.

"Simply this, my friend, that cities are very much like men. Some are born great, others achieve greatness, while still others have greatness thrust upon them. In any and all of these cases there must be a certain degree of fitness enabling them to endure this greatness; while in none of them can greatness be manufactured and the town then be thrust into it; and this, it strikes me, is the very thing you are trying to do."

"I don't see what has come to you, Mitchell," Warren answered, rather crossly, crumbling his bread nervously as he spoke.

"What I wish had come to you," he answered, "a rational and common-sense way of looking at things. It would have been dollars and cents in your pocket had you been inoculated with this worldly wisdom before you embarked in this scheme."

Then, interrupting Warren, who was about to return a sharp answer, he added,—

"I beg your pardon, Warren, but hear me out. You will notice that in every one of these towns which have suddenly come up from little or nothing into flourishing places, there is a reason for this marvellous development. There is either a wonderfully rich soil, or there is a great fruit or wine industry to support the place, or, as in Los Angeles and San Diego, they are commercial centres; or else, like Ventura, they possess a productive soil themselves, with a fertile country back of them whose products they handle and ship. The reason for growth is there, you see; they are none of them, strictly speaking, boom towns. While the scenery, climate, and so on are there too, yet these are thrown in gratis, no extra charge. I don't want to throw cold water on your scheme, but it seems to me to be one of those enterprises which are founded on nothing but scenery and climate, so common out here, which already have brought reproach on the country, and which are, from their very beginning, destined to come to naught."

"Thank you, Mitchell, thank you," Warren answered, hotly, highly indignant with his plainly-speaking friend. "If Job had three such comforters as you, he should have been canonized by the church centuries ago. Human sanctity can know no higher perfection than that patience and forbearance which prevented his falling upon them and strangling them to the last man."

"I beg pardon if I have hurt you; I only want you

to know how I look at the matter; and I think that this is the light in which any disinterested and cool-headed person would view it," Mitchell replied.

Further discussion was prevented by the resumption of the sale. All through the afternoon the bidding went on; and, under the graphic word-painting of the auctioneer, where now were only open lots, oak-trees, and sage-brush, fancy could picture massive business blocks, with the elegant homes and picturesque villas of wealthy merchants, shaded by palms, magnolias, and fig-trees.

The bidding was more brisk and spirited than in the morning; and at the close of the sale Warren triumphantly announced that over forty-five thousand dollars' worth of lots had been sold.

"Your auctioneer understood his business and did his best to serve your interests; he has fairly earned his percentage," Mitchell answered.

"Yes; but what more nearly concerns you is the fact that you had best make haste to the train, or you will earn the privilege of standing up all the way back to town," Warren replied.

But for all the apparently handsome success which the sale had achieved, something was manifestly wrong, for Warren had hardly finished speaking before Glenn came up with an anxious look on his face, took Warren by the arm, and whispered in his ear.

"I cannot do it, I have a friend with me. It is out of the question, and you must wait till to-morrow," Warren emphatically replied, his voice and manner betraying the utmost annoyance and vexation.

"To-morrow will not do; you must stay," Glenn answered, in a tone as positive as Warren's had been.

12

Mollie quickly saw that she was concerned in this debate, and coming forward, she said,—

"Mr. Glenn, if you wish to detain Mr. Warren for business purposes, I can return on the train with my brother and sister if you will see that my horse is safely taken back to town."

"Thank you, Miss Wade," Glenn replied. "It is of great importance that Mr. Warren should remain to a meeting of the stockholders of the company; and, as for your horse, my little niece will take it back safely. She is a great horsewoman, so you need feel no fear in trusting her; and, being a child, a habit is not necessary. She will think the ride a great treat."

"This is outrageous," Warren said, under his breath, to his companion, as Glenn hurried away. "I fear that you will never accept me as an escort again."

Mollie laughed merrily at his annoyance at the unexpected disarrangement of his plans, and answered,—

"Be a hero, Mr. Warren, and do not let trifles so seriously vex you. Of course I should have been glad of the ride back, and I should have also enjoyed your companionship; but for this once I shall survive the loss of both. You are not in the least responsible for this turn of affairs, and I hope you do not think I regard you so. I thank you for giving me a very pleasant day, and at any time when you are ready for another excursion, I shall be most happy to go with you. Good-night!" And taking her brother's arm she tripped away to the train, leaving Warren standing and looking after her, and thinking that night had fallen over the scene two full hours before its time.

CHAPTER X.

SOMETHING, it was clearly to be seen by the most superficial observer, was altogether wrong. What this "something" was could not so easily be ascertained, for the sales had certainly been good ; the bidding had been fairly spirited ; but for all this, after the adjournment of their informal meeting, not a member of the Oakdale Company left the grounds with a countenance expressive of the satisfaction which every one of them ought to have felt at the termination of so successful a sale.

Whether this arose from the fact that these enterprising speculators were anxious to control the entire planet upon which they dwelt and would be satisfied · with nothing less, or whether there was some mystery behind the whole affair at present known only to the stockholders, no one could say, for those in the secret carefully kept their own counsel.

"Be at the office at nine to-morrow, promptly," said Glenn, the president of the company, as he climbed into his carriage.

"I will," Warren answered.

"Every one of us must be on hand ; this matter cannot wait." With these words Glenn drove off home, the others scattered, and the impromptu meeting of the Oakdale Company stood adjourned.

Warren mounted his horse and rode thoughtfully and sadly towards Ventura. The journey home was by no means as pleasant to him as the ride of the morning had been, and he found the companionship of his thoughts by no means as pleasant as the society of his pretty friend had proved a few brief hours before. His horse was a good one, but so slowly did he ride that the sun had long gone down and twilight had come on before he had reached the narrow pass which marked the half-way point between the Oakdale tract and town.

As he had been almost the last to leave the grounds and, intent upon his own thoughts, had ridden very slowly, the other attendants at the sale—stockholders, speculators, and spectators—had gone through the pass long before he reached it.

It was a beautiful and romantic spot by daylight; but it was dark, gloomy, and (except to a skilful driver) dangerous after nightfall. On one side the hills towered up over the road, their precipitous sides covered with a thick growth of oak. On the other a sheer descent of hundreds of feet led down into a cañon, narrow and crooked, opening off a broad valley through which a clear stream wound its way down to the ocean. This cañon in former days, when the valley had been a famous range for cattle, had been used as a corral into which cattle were driven for branding, for herding, and for selecting stock for the markets. The old corral was now, however, in no way useful or interesting except for the old associations and weird traditions connected with it.

A cowboy, so it was said, had long ago been murdered in it by a treacherous companion; and he was popularly supposed to have the poor taste to still linger around the scene of his former labors and final sufferings. On moonlight nights he had often been seen to ride a ghostly horse in pursuit of ghostly cattle, swinging a ghostly lasso around his head as he drove his spectral charge into the old corral.

Warren, however, being in perfect health and possessed of a good digestion, was distressed by no fears of being granted a glimpse at this vision of the supernatural ; but the sight which was revealed to him as he approached that part of the pass overhanging the old corral was little less of a shock to him than that he would have received had he actually seen the spectre horseman "rounding up" his immaterial herds hundreds of feet below.

On the road just above the old corral two men were engaged in a contest of life and death ; while their horses, left to their own devices, were silently browsing by the road and calmly indifferent to the enmity of their masters, which could evidently end only with the life of one, while perhaps it would cost the lives of both.

Firmly clasped in an embrace of mortal hatred, they were swaying back and forth, now in the middle of the road, now almost on the edge of the cañon. Both were powerful men, both manifested a spirit of terrible determination, and every inch of ground was fought with a desperate strength and courage which showed that the battle would end with only one of them standing upon the road, though Warren feared that neither would survive the quarrel.

Now they were on the very edge of the precipice, and one of the antagonists, slighter and more athletic in his build, had almost forced his foe over the brink. With feet firmly braced, he struggled to detach his adversary's hands from their firm clasp about his waist, then force him on the few inches necessary to hurl him to his death. But the brief pause necessary to accomplish this cost him all the advantage that he had gained. Back, inch by inch, he was forced from the edge of the precipice; and still struggling to unclasp the clinging arms wound around him, the more athletic of the two again forced his enemy on to the edge of the chasm, forcing him once more, inch by inch, on to his death.

With an exclamation of horror, Warren put spurs to his horse and dashed up to the spot, calling out to the wrestlers as he flew over the ground. The road was very narrow at this point, and as he reached the place the fight was once more going on upon the very edge of the precipice, while both the participators were in imminent danger of going over its edge in each other's deadly embrace.

Warren sprang from his horse upon reaching them, and, catching each by the collar, he tore them from one another, saying,—

"Gently, gently, let us have no more of this! Good heavens, Jake, is this you? Will you have the kindness to tell me what this exhibition of Græco-Roman wrestling means?" he added, as he recognized his friend in one of the combatants.

Still holding each by the collar he looked from one to the other, while his captives, gasping for breath from the violence of their late exertions, stood perfectly quiet and made no resistance to his interference, looking him calmly in the face.

By the dim light of the early evening he did not

recognize in Jake's antagonist any one whom he had ever seen before. Leaning forward and peering into his face, he found that the man was an entire stranger, though his dark complexion told Warren that he was of Spanish or Mexican descent.

"Could you not have found some more secure place for your gymnastic entertainments,—some spot, for instance, where your diversions would not be so likely to become varied by exhibitions of your skill in ground and lofty tumbling?" Warren again asked, after looking at his prisoners a moment in silence.

The Mexican was the first to recover his breath, and, throwing off Warren's detaining grasp, he stepped back, saying, in perfect English, though with a strong foreign accent,—

"The señor chooses to be witty, but I assure him that nothing could be in more deadly earnest than the contest upon which he happened so inopportunely."

"I beg leave to differ with you as to that point," Warren answered, releasing Jake as he spoke, but carefully keeping himself between them. "It seems to me that my arrival was most fortunate, for it has very clearly prevented the commission of a crime, while it has not improbably prevented the destruction of you both. May I trouble you for an explanation?"

The Mexican shrugged his shoulders, but made no other reply, though his manner clearly intimated that he continued to look upon Warren's interference as an unwarrantable intrusion into matters that did not in the least concern him. Jake, however, although he was still sadly out of breath, attempted to give Warren an understanding of the situation, and replied,—

"I give you my word for it, Mr. Warren, this row ain't none of my doin's. Carballo would have it, though, and of course I started in to take good care of number one."

The name enlightened Warren at once. The fight was clearly connected with Jake's love-affair, and this young Spaniard (as he proved to be), the young lady's brother, had evidently made up his mind to free his sister from the attentions of a lover who was so unacceptable to the family, even if it were necessary to terminate the engagement by putting an end to his life. Turning to the young Spaniard, on hearing this answer, Warren asked,—

"Are you the Señor Carballo?"

"That is my name," he answered, very coolly, brushing the dust from his clothes as he spoke.

"Did this disgraceful affair originate with you?" Warren sternly demanded.

"That is a matter of opinion altogether. You can only arrive at a just conclusion as to the merits of the case by reasoning from cause to effect," Carballo answered, as coolly as before.

Warren was exasperated by his calm insolence, and angrily replied,—

"Come, sir, you will gain nothing by this evasion. I have witnessed an attempt at crime on your part, remember; and it would be well for you to bear in mind that the authorities of the county would call your crime by a very ugly name. If you can give me any reason why I should not lodge an information against you with them, now is your time."

"I have nothing to say to you, señor. If the authorities have any questions to ask of me they will always know where to find me, and I will recognize their right to inquire," Carballo answered, seizing his horse's bridle and preparing to mount.

Evidently he was a cool hand, a very cool hand, indeed, and one who was not to be easily frightened. So Warren decided within himself, but he determined to make one more effort towards bringing him to reason before he let him go, and called out to him saying,—

"Stop a moment, señor! It may be that I understand more of this matter than you suspect. I have no desire to drag a young lady's name into unpleasant publicity; but before I can consent to drop this matter I must have your promise to attempt no further unlawful violence."

Carballo stood silent for a moment, his graceful and powerful form dimly outlined in the growing darkness against the background of his horse. Then he answered, with bitter sarcasm in his voice,—

"When you wish to clear your house of vermin, do you first go to the courts and secure their license?"

On hearing himself alluded to in such uncomplimentary language, Jake gave vent to a half-stifled oath and sprang forward to take vengeance of his prospective brother-in-law.

Warren at once seized him and drew him back, saying,—

"Jake, behave yourself!" Then, turning to Carballo, he said,—

"My friend, in all civilized communities there is a peculiar disposition, to you I suppose wholly unaccountable, which is strongly in favor of protecting human life. I would invite your attention to the fact that this is now a civilized section; the laws now have a force out here, and the sentiment of the people endorses this love of law and order. If anything happens to my young friend here, you will, after this evening's demonstration, be held accountable; and I greatly fear that the results to you will be a throat-trouble of short but violent nature, whose termination will certainly prove fatal."

Carballo sprang into the saddle, and, bowing low in mock courtesy, said, in reply,—

"I thank you, señor, for your deep interest in my welfare. I have been charmed by your eloquence and entertained by your wit. I now commend your interesting friend to your protection; believe me, he will need all your care. *Buenos noches.*" And, raising his hat, he rode away.

"That is a cool fellow and no mistake," Warren said, looking after Carballo as he vanished in the darkness. Then turning to his companion, he said,—

"Well, Jake, I think it would be as well for us to follow the example of our late entertaining friend and decamp. I suppose, as I hinted to Carballo, a certain fair maiden was the remote cause of the gymnastic exercises I beheld as I came up?"

"Yes," Jake answered, as they mounted. "He was waitin' for me in the pass here; and as I came up he called to me and asked me to dismount, as he wanted to talk to me. I did so, and we got into hot words; then he took hold of me, and we went at it hot and heavy."

"He certainly meant to release his sister from her

engagement, didn't he ?" Warren asked, laughing as he spoke.

"I rather think that his family were just as likely to go into mourning on his account," Jake answered, grimly.

"In that case he would have gained his purpose just the same, for the fair señorita could hardly have married the man who killed her brother," Warren replied.

"It would have been all right if I had ; he pitched into me, I didn't go for him," Jake argued.

"True enough ; but then the principle holds good, and would have prevented such a marriage just the same ; however, all's well that ends well. I am glad that I came up in time ; only, I beg of you, don't get into any more such scrapes if you can help it," Warren answered.

"How can I help it if he comes along and hunts me up in order to pitch into me ? You wouldn't have me stand still and let him cut my throat, would you ?" Jake protested.

"Hardly," Warren returned. "I cordially commend all the efforts you put forth in the way of self-defence. All I meant was, to caution you against putting yourself in his way, or doing anything to provoke trouble. Meanwhile, I shall see the young man again and take measures to effectually curb his warlike propensities for the future."

"I am glad that you came up as you did, Mr. Warren," said Jake. "But I shall put an end to this whole business for good and all."

"What are you going to do ?" Warren asked, anxiously.

"I don't know just yet," Jake replied, "but I shall do something right away."

"Don't follow the example of our friend and be violent," Warren cautioned.

Jake laughed and answered,—

"I am not a Spaniard; you need not fear that I shall try to exterminate the family, and I sha'n't stand any nonsense from them, either. I'll let you know in a few days what I'm up to."

"All right, only don't be rash," Warren cautioned again.

Having by this time reached the city, they rode to the stable and there parted, Jake to go home, Warren to go to the hotel, get his supper, and then spend the small portion of the evening still remaining to him in the society of his friends.

CHAPTER XI.

WARREN did not sleep well that night, either owing to his business troubles or to the excitement of his adventure in the pass; and the pleasant evening he had passed in Mollie's society did not serve to overcome the restlessness which one or the other of these causes, or perhaps the combined influence of both, had exercised over his spirits. Weary in body and mind, but wholly unable to sleep, he tossed uneasily on his pillow through the entire night, anxiously watching for the first break of day, which he welcomed with the joy only those can feel who have, like him, been unwilling watchers through a long and weary night. The first pale gray of the morning twilight called Warren from his bed; and after first trying to read, then making an equally futile attempt at letter-writing, he threw aside pen and paper with an exclamation of impatience.

"It's of no use," he said, angry with himself, and tearing up his epistolary failure as he spoke. "No tea-drinking old maid was ever more nervous and altogether unstrung than I am at this present moment. What has come over me anyway? This Oakdale business? That little *fiasco* in the pass on the way home? It does not seem as though it could be either of these; for any man who is a man at all ought to be able to bear trouble or excitement without turning womanish, and I do not seem to be so much worried as altogether unstrung."

Going to the window, he looked out over the glorious sunshine which was now painting mountains and coastline, islands and ocean with the rich orange and gold of early day; and, inhaling the sweet fragrance of the morning air, filled with the cool invigorating perfume of the sea, he took up his hat and cane, saying,—

"I believe I will try a walk. I am no great worshipper of Aurora, but if the goddess of the dawn ever did cure an attack of the 'blues,' she certainly ought to be able to do something for me, aided, as she is, by such grand scenery and refreshing breezes, while I am a fit subject for her kindly attentions. One thing, though, is a fact: a long walk will at least serve to take up the time between now and the breakfast hour."

For the first time in his life Warren went out to make trial of the fresh air and bright sunshine of early day as a remedy for unstrung nerves; and being determined to make thorough work of it, he aimed for the steepest and highest of the foot-hills, intending to climb to its summit for his morning walk. He had not gone more than two blocks along Poli Street in this direction when his attention was attracted by a young lady sauntering along only a little distance before him, with the easy bearing of one whose sole errand was the enjoyment of a pleasant walk with happy thoughts and good health for her company.

Warren felt certain that he recognized the mountain dress and modish hat, so becoming to the trim figure and pretty face which had already played such sad havoc with his heart. But could it be that Miss Wade, whom he knew to be a "society girl," could it be that she was out of her bed and walking in the open air at so very unfashionable an hour?

He hastened his steps in order to make sure. Yes, it certainly was she; he could not be mistaken. The bearing, the poise of the pretty head, the graceful gliding motion; he could not be mistaken; no other girl of his acquaintance knew *how* to walk.

In a few moments he was close behind her, almost at her side. Yes, he was right, as he had all along known that he must be; and she, hearing his steps, turned her head to see who was following her with such a very evident desire to overtake her.

Mollie's countenance expressed her surprise at seeing him, and, bidding him a laughing good-morning, she waited the second necessary to permit him to join her.

"This *is* an unexpected pleasure, Mr. Warren," she cried, throwing a strong emphasis upon the monosyllabic verb. "What fascination is at work sufficiently powerful to draw you from your bed at this early hour, when you are usually taking your beauty sleep?"

"I am the one to express surprise, Miss Wade," Warren answered. "Who would ever dream of finding a fashionable young lady forsaking her bed to enjoy a constitutional at sunrise? Is this a regular practice with you?"

"It is," Mollie replied. "But permit me to caution you, Mr. Warren, not to indulge yourself with any railing against 'fashionable young ladies' in my presence. I know very well that I am possessed of an exceptionally sweet temper and an almost perfect disposition; but even these perfections are not proof against that most absurd of all absurdities, the foolish cry against 'fashionable girls.' Please tell me what you mean when you define the term."

Warren had not been expecting to be taken up in this way and so suddenly brought to book; for a moment he looked puzzled, and then hesitatingly answered,—

"Why—I—I—should say that a fashionable girl is one who gives up her time and her thoughts altogether to society."

"Oh, should you?" was Mollie's scornful reply. "Do *you* know any such girl, Mr. Warren? I confess that there are none of that description in the circle of my acquaintance. Indeed, I cannot imagine such a girl. One whose whole life was passed in gayety, with no home life, no religious life, no life of any kind outside of this one whirl of amusement, would be a strange creature, would she not?"

"Of course I did not intend that you should place a strictly literal interpretation upon my words," Warren replied. "Of course a girl must possess some kind of domestic instincts, more or less perfectly developed, however ill-defined her moral and religious ideas may be. What I meant by my definition was, that my idea of a fashionable girl is, one who makes her social success the chief end and aim of her existence."

"I perfectly understood your meaning, Mr. Warren," Mollie answered; "and I intended to show you that your definition would not bear inspection even a moment."

"Where is its flaw?" Warren asked, disposed to feel hurt at her criticism.

"It is fatally defective in its every word, as I will

show you in just one moment," Mollie replied, as she stooped over a bed of California poppies to add their yellow glory to the bouquet of wild-flowers she was carrying in her hand. "There," she said, rising with her new treasures; "is not that lovely? Lupines; wild onions,—though I think it is a shame to call such a pretty blue flower by such a horrible name; Mariposas,—*they* are rightly named, though, with the butterfly beauty of their painted petals; and now I have these rich yellow poppies to set it all off as it should be. The fields have given me a more beautiful bouquet than I could have found outside of a conservatory at home. Did you ever see anything more lovely in your life?" she asked, standing before her companion and holding up her flowers for his approval.

"I never saw anything that I thought one-half so beautiful," Warren returned, somewhat dishonestly, it must be confessed, looking not at the flowers but at the face uplifted to his own.

It was a face well worth looking upon: the pure, clear complexion glowing with health; the bright, dark eyes sparkling with happiness and animation; the red, dewy lips parted just enough to show the pearly teeth beneath, all combined to form a lovely picture, and Warren can almost be pardoned his wicked evasion of her question. She caught his meaning instantly and dropped her eyes, flushing slightly as she answered his apparent instead of his real meaning, saying,—

"Yes, I think that I have almost a genius for arranging flowers. But I must not forget my duty of remorselessly tearing in pieces your definition, which

13*

my soul abhors. Your majesty has graciously deigned
to admit that your ‘fashionable girl’ *must* give some
little of her time and thoughts to something besides
her social life; but still she is too frivolous. Now,
your definition fails to define in this: how is one to
know whether a girl is ‘fashionable’ or not? Are we,
who wish to escape this dreadful condemnation, to
dress ourselves like guys, and behave ourselves altogether in defiance of social laws?”

“Why, certainly not!” Warren answered, shocked
at the very idea.

“Then, what are we to do?” Mollie insisted. “If
we girls are all alike to dress and do as social laws
direct, who of us can touch this awful pitch, ‘*fashion*,’
without being defiled? And you have just called me a
‘fashionable girl’ too.”

This last she said in a tone expressive of the deepest
reproach. Warren felt that Mollie was almost unjust
in pressing so closely a speech that had been inadver-
tent on his part, and which he had not intended should
possess any great amount of significance; while he certainly had not intended her to understand that he regarded her as in the slightest degree frivolous, or that
he thought any one could so regard her, and he at once
hastened to reply:

“Oh, Miss Mollie, I assure you that I did not use
the phrase in its conventional and uncomplimentary
sense; quite the contrary, in fact.”

Mollie laughed heartily at his distressed countenance,
and answered,—

“Thank you very much for your graceful compliment. But seriously, Mr. Warren, I do object very

strongly to that ridiculous phrase, 'fashionable girl.' We are all of us fashionable girls," she went on, with a look of intense earnestness in her bright, pretty face; "that is, all of us are who are good for anything. Society and the ideas that other people entertain have rights which we are bound to respect, and they make certain righteous demands upon us which we are bound to meet and honor; and those of us who defy these demands are just as selfish in one way as those are in another way who live only to themselves."

"That is true," Warren answered; "and the young ladies I intended to describe by the phrase in using which I was so unhappy as to provoke your indignation are the large class of girls who have no thoughts above nice and becoming gowns and the pretty graces by which they hope to shine as bright particular stars in the fashionable world."

Mollie glanced quickly at her companion with a very serious look in her dark eyes; and, giving an emphatic shake of her graceful head, she answered,—

"I cannot permit that censure to pass unchallenged either. You have no right to say of any girl that she has no thought beyond social success. Now, I am no better (and I hope I am no worse) than other girls of my set; but in our parish at home we girls have a guild, every member of which is one of those dreadful creatures you have just been condemning,—a 'fashionable girl.' Besides other religious duties, we pledge ourselves to give one-tenth of our income for pious purposes, while over and above this we give as we are able to the support of the parish. We also teach in a mission Sunday-school, while we also do district visit-

ing under the direction of the Sisters. The world
knows nothing of all this, though. We cannot go
around telling every one what we do; it would be im-
modest and irreligious; then, it is just no one's business but our own and our rector's. So, I have no
doubt that you, and every one else who knows nothing
about us and our motives, set down every individual
member of this guild as a girl wholly given over to the
pomps and vanities of this sinful world, and as being
possessed of a mind incapable of rising above follies
and fripperies. And why, pray? Just because she
tries to fulfil her duties to society when she is in society
just as loyally as she does every other duty, and to this
end makes herself just as bright and attractive as she
can. But, Mr. Warren," she added, mischievously,
"it is worthy of remark that, like every other con-
temner of the 'fashionable girl,' at every ball and
reception given this season, where there were two girls
present who were, physically, equally attractive, you
have always inconsistently chosen as your partner the
better dressed, better mannered, and therefore more
'fashionable' of the two."

Warren laughed heartily at her vigorous defence of
a much-maligned class of the fair sex.

"I acknowledge myself defeated," he said, "and
I confess that you have given me many new ideas and
a new insight into feminine character and motives;
while I must also admit that I am no match for you
in debate. You should have studied law, Miss Mollie;
you are far better qualified for the profession than I."

"Oh, no," she replied; "I claim no skill in argument at all. But, as you have just admitted, you saw

that you were in the wrong, and were too fair to try to make the worse appear the better reason."

"Oh, thank you," said Warren. "All the bitterness is taken from my defeat, because I am overcome by an antagonist so fair, so valiant, and so generous in victory. But have you not forgotten to tell me if you are always so early a riser?"

"I think not. I am certain that I did assure you of the fact that it is my custom to rise with the sun and refresh myself with a brisk walk on every pleasant day."

"Of course, like all such frightfully energetic people, you are in pursuit of health?" Warren said, interrogatively.

"Oh, certainly; I am seeking neither wisdom nor riches, having already all I desire of either, and certainly all that I can make a good use of; but health is the one thing with which no one can be overblessed," Mollie answered.

"What do you do to dispose of days which you lengthen so unconscionably?" Warren asked, as they turned to retrace their steps to the hotel.

"I find enough to keep me busy," she replied. "First, I always go back with a ravenous appetite, and eat a hearty breakfast. You cannot imagine how thankful I have always been that, since the steward placed you at our table, you were not an early riser. I should certainly have shocked you beyond description with my appetite at breakfast; while I feel a humiliating consciousness that my prowess has dismayed you sufficiently as it is. After breakfast there are always letters to be written, errands to be done, either for my-

self or for Effie; and then, when all else fails, there is
the never-failing feminine resource, fancy work, at
hand to occupy spare moments that need to be supplied with duties, while you have no need to ask how
many hours a week I consume in riding. No, Mr.
Warren; I see the question in your face, and I will
forestall it. I *do not* perpetrate any of those grotesque
horrors which young ladies now burlesque art by calling 'paintings.' As for the amateurish scrawls which
I call drawings, the less said about them the better I
shall feel, especially after what *you* said about them,
you know, on our ride to the Ojai," she added, with a
teasing glance into his face. Then she continued,—

"I simply detest sewing, and I do not do any when
I can avoid it. But here we are; and, while I have
enjoyed my walk, I think that I ought to extend you
my heartiest sympathy at having been inflicted with my
company during yours, for I *have* talked, to be sure.
I have just so much to say every morning, and you
have been compelled to pay the penalty of meeting me
before I had exhausted my powers upon Effie and John
Addison."

Warren did not tell her, what would have been the
truth, that he loved above all things else to hear her
voice, or say that it was, to him, the sweetest music in
the world, simply because he did not dare to do so;
while fortune still further favored him this morning
by permitting him to enjoy a *tête-à-tête* breakfast with
her, neither Mitchell nor his wife coming down while
they were at the table.

"Mr. Warren," Mollie said, as they seated themselves,
"I want to tell you that you are deserving of great

credit for what you did on your way home from the sale last evening."

Warren's pulse beat more quickly than usual; for never, since their acquaintance began, had she spoken to him in so cordial a tone.

"Don't overrate a trifling act such as that; where there is no possible danger there can be no heroism displayed. Whatever might have happened to Elkins had I not come upon the field as I did, my interposition did not imperil my existence in the least," Warren answered.

"You have been a true friend to that young man ever since you have known him, and a valuable friend as well," she added.

"Why, I did not suppose that you knew anything of my relations to him," Warren answered, surprised at her information concerning himself and his doings, but happy because she did know and appreciate it.

"John Addison has told me all about it," she replied. "If you want to keep your proceedings secret, never let him find out anything. I fear he is a terrible gossip."

"Don't let him persuade you into believing that I am a philanthropist, Miss Wade. I am by no means given to going around the world seeking out whom I may aid," Warren said, as he glanced at his watch and then rose from the table, finding that it was now time for him to be on the way to his office.

Mollie laughed as she answered,—

"That is not always the truest philanthropy, Mr. Warren. Was it not Sir John Suckling who said of love, 'It is of the nature of a burning-glass, which, kept still in one place, fireth; changed often, it doeth nothing'? And something of the same sort is true of our love to our fellows which makes us ready to help them; we have to keep our kindly interest fixed in one place and make that the scene of our activity, and help those who need help as they come into it; for if we try to spread our sympathetic feelings over the whole world, our good deeds are very likely to begin and end in nothing but feeling; and it strikes me that you are trying to act according to this good rule."

" I have certainly done nothing as yet deserving of praise or even of notice," Warren answered, as he bade her good-morning. Although he so strongly disavowed the performance of any meritorious action, he was made very happy, all the same, by the commendation she had given him. He felt that he must certainly be more worthy in her sight than he had once been, for never before had she been so cordial with him as she had shown herself this morning.

A sudden change from day to night, from midsummer to midwinter, is never pleasant, but just such a change it seemed to Warren that he was making as he left Mollie to walk down to his office for the purpose of attending a business meeting which, as he had been forewarned, was called to discuss nothing less than loss, while it was quite possible that it might have to deal with disaster.

The four stockholders of the Oakdale company were present,—Glenn, Warren, a New York man named, or misnamed, West, while the last member of the corporation hailed from San Francisco; and considering the shearing process to which he was destined to be sub-

jected, he rejoiced in the highly appropriate name of
Lamb. Glenn, as president and manager of the company, opened the proceedings by saying,—

"I am sorry to be obliged to tell you that our sale
of yesterday was a flat failure, and we shall have to do
something—take some positive action—at once, or this
company will certainly go to the wall."

"I thought that the lots went off nicely, and that
we were making a pretty good thing out of it. For
the life of me I can't see where you figure in the loss
and how you bring us into such a desperate situation,"
Warren replied.

Glenn looked compassionately upon his partner, as
upon one altogether too guileless to fathom the plots
and counterplots of the business world, and then
answered,—

"We shall never see any money for a good share of
those lots. They were bid off by agents I had employed to keep up the prices and prevent the whole
sale from falling flat."

Warren flushed hotly at this frank confession of a
double game, his ideas of integrity and his partner's
theories of business enterprise by no means coinciding.
The other stockholders also seemed to view the trans-
action from Warren's stand-point, and appeared a trifle
uneasy. Glenn saw the sensation his open avowal had
created, and, turning to Warren, he said,—

"See here, my friend, for a man of your years, and
for one who has so good a legal education, I never in
all my life set eyes on one with such crude ideas of
business and so full of finicky notions as you are.
If you are going to make a success in this live part

14

of the world, you've got to get rid of your nonsense and get a little *go* into you."

"It may be that this affair strikes Mr. Warren and myself in the same light," Mr. West remarked.

"I hope that your ideas of *go* didn't prompt you to put up a stool-pigeon game at this sale," Mr. Lamb interposed.

Glenn glanced angrily from one to the other of the speakers, his small sharp eyes glistening like needles as he answered,—

"Everything connected with the sale was perfectly open and above-board. But I kept my eyes open, gentlemen. I knew that there was going to be a snap game sprung on us from some quarter or other. I had got wind of that scheme (no matter how) which was being put up to cry down our property and represent us as acting in bad faith; so, when that white-livered hound got up and bayed at us, if I hadn't been all primed and loaded and ready for him, we'd have had to come sneaking back home like a lot of whipped young ones, snivelling along with our fingers in our mouths. We wouldn't have sold a lot, gentlemen, if it hadn't been for me. Not a single, blessed lot!"

"I should judge from what you say that the fellow threw cold water on us pretty effectually for all your sharpness," said Mr. Lamb.

"Rather!" Glenn angrily replied. "We shall have small money coming in. When we balance our accounts you'll find that most of the lots were bid back to the company; and they wouldn't have sold as well as they did if I hadn't fixed things beforehand, and if we hadn't been lucky enough to get a bang-up auctioneer as well."

"I can't understand why it is that we are meeting so much opposition," said Mr. West, anxiously. "We are not opposing any one on our side, and why should other companies try to cut our throats?"

"It's rivalry! it's just the narrow-minded, short-sighted, pig-headedness of some dealers right here in this town!" Glenn roared, fairly beside himself with anger, and banging his fist on the table before him in his fury as he spoke. "These stupid fools are afraid that everything that don't come directly into town is going to hurt the town. They haven't got brains enough to see that what builds up the county can't help building up the town. And now I've got a blister ready which I want to show you, then I shall proceed to put it on."

With these words he unrolled a closely-written manuscript and read as follows:

"The Oakdale Land and Water Company, To all barking curs, snarling jackals, and sneaking coyotes who are laboring for its demise in order to devour its remains, greeting:

"From the time that the Oakdale Land and Water Company was first organized up to the present day there has been a confederacy composed of a number of leering, lying, sneaking individuals, who have done everything in their power to crush the enterprise. They not only try to depreciate the property by insinuations, they even deliberately lie. Every few weeks some fiendish, malevolent scoundrel will bark at the company, and all the mongrel curs of low degree will join in the yelping, discordant chorus.

"Instead of admitting facts,—that Oakdale is a part

of this wonderful county ; that it possesses advantages in some respects unsurpassed by any other section of the State, or even of this grand globe, illuminated by the golden ball of the great orb of day,—these vindictive, splenetic individuals will lie about it so that the uninformed would think that the wilds of Sahara were a fertile oasis compared with it.

"Or, if the location be admitted to be good, the honesty of the company is assailed. The company don't mean what it says. It is organized for no purpose but just to shear innocent lambs. It is incompetent to meet its obligations. It has always been insolvent, and the fools who have bought property from it will lose every cent they have invested. Lying assertions are these, all of them ; but it is a sad fact that a lie will travel leagues while truth is putting on its boots.

"We defy any man to come out into the broad light of day, so that we can see him and know him, and dare to say that the Oakdale Company has not met every obligation it has ever assumed, and we guarantee to cram his infamous lie down his scurrilous throat.

"When has the Oakdale Company wronged a man of a dollar ? When has it failed to meet, and promptly, every obligation ? Let the Solomon who knows come out from his hypocritical concealment and speak, that we may know him.

"Let him be manly !'

"Let him throw off his contemptible, cowardly, stab-in-the-back demeanor and be an open enemy ; then we will respect him. But an assassin, a cowardly, cringing cur, we detest.

"The Oakdale Land and Water Company will in the future, as in the past, pay every dollar that it owes, and faithfully meet every agreement. It has developed a splendid property. It has secured railroad facilities through which the back country can find an easy and profitable market for. its abounding harvests. The depot will be built at once and a post-office will shortly be established, while the silurians will be quietly restored to their ancient geological formations to wait for the next scheme for advancing the prosperity of the country to call forth their croaks.

"To these slanderous fossils, whose chief occupation it is to wear smooth the seat of their pants by physical inaction ; to these specimens of a low order of animal life who would rather a whole train of progress would run over them than strain their incomplete organism by getting out of the way ; to these inhuman specimens of crude creation which ages of evolution cannot raise to the dignity of the baboon we direct these remarks. If any have doubts as to their identity, we let them know that we can establish it, and we withhold their names now not through consideration for them, but out of respect for ourselves.

"Some of them call themselves business men ; though what business they ever transact, unless they call slander and backbiting a legitimate occupation, we have never been able to learn.

"We regret that such cannibalistic character-eaters and lying detractors can exist in this glorious State ; and above all do we regret the. presence of such reptiles in that unequalled, beautiful, and progressive part of it lying south of Point Conception."

l 14*

Glenn laid down his manuscript and looked around upon his hearers with the self-satisfied manner of a man whose pent-up feelings have found a safety-valve just in time to prevent an explosion dangerous alike to himself and to all his associates.

"There," he said, tilting back in his chair; "that will touch up somebody right smart. The blister will fit on just where it belongs. Now, the question for us to decide is, where shall we insert it?"

"I think the best and most fitting place to insert that production is the stove," Mr. West quietly suggested, as he cut the end from a cigar and slowly proceeded to light it. Lamb said nothing, but nodded his approval of his colleague's suggestion.

Once more the darkness of a coming storm began to gather upon Glenn's brow. He glared upon the presumptuous speaker for a moment in threatening silence, transfixing him with an awful look, intended to strike terror into his soul, but which West's calm and untroubled demeanor proclaimed to have altogether failed in its intention; then he said, in a voice trembling with ill-suppressed fury,—

"Well, sir, what fault have you to find with this letter? I called you here for suggestions, and if you have any to make I shall be happy to hear them."

"I meant no offence, Mr. Glenn," West replied. "But that letter doesn't strike me as at all a dignified production, and it reads as though it had been written in anger. If it is published it will turn the laugh on us by showing every one that, for all our grand splurge, we got wretchedly left at the sale; and it will increase whatever distrust there may be felt towards us by the anger it shows. Those on the winning side never lose their temper; so, if we use printer's ink at all, I would advise that we publish a calm, temperate statement of facts, and invite any one who wishes to do so to investigate our financial condition and inspect our books."

"Never !" Glenn roared, once more pounding the table with his fist. "While I am president of this company it shall never be investigated by a lot of sneaking and lying silurians."

"I think myself that will be the easiest way out of the hole we are in, Glenn; it will show our good faith," Warren interposed, trying to soothe his irate partner into a better and more reasonable temper.

Glenn was now almost beside himself with anger.

"I will permit nothing of the kind !" he howled, jumping out of his chair and kicking it into a corner, then turning around to glare at his companions.

"Oh, that I have lived to see the day that I should have to do business in company with a pack of moss-backed antediluvians ! *You* business men ! *You* a lawyer, Warren ! There isn't one of you that has the faintest idea how to do business. You are a pack of mealy-mouthed milksops; you are a lot of half-weaned tenderfeet; and if we go to the wall, you have sent us there, and you'll have no one but yourselves to blame."

With these words he picked up his hat, crushed it down on his head, and rushed out of the office to walk off his wrath on the street.

For a few moments the remaining supporters of the unfortunate Oakdale enterprise sat looking upon one another in silence; then Mr. Lamb arose, and, picking up his hat, said,—

"Well, I shall have just about time to walk down to the wharf and catch the boat for Frisco. I guess I'll go that way, it's cheaper; and, from the ideas I gather from this meeting in regard to our affairs, I should say that we shall all of us need to be careful of our money. Have you any positive knowledge as to how we stand, Mr. Warren?"

Warren shook his head dubiously as he answered,—

"No, Mr. Lamb, I have not the shadow of an idea. Glenn is the treasurer of the company, as well as its president and manager, and he has never submitted to me any statement of its affairs or invited me to go over the books. You are as well informed as to its condition as I am."

"I should think that the sale was a perfect fizzle, everything considered, and that we are in danger of going to everlasting smash," Mr. West remarked.

"I think nothing will save us but a heavy assessment," Warren replied.

"I, for one, will never consent to that!" was West's emphatic answer to this hint.

"For another, I will never put one cent more into this scheme than I have already invested in it," said Mr. Lamb, in his turn; and, bidding them good-day, he left the office and wended his way to the wharf.

"As the meeting is evidently adjourned, I may as well be going, for there is nothing that you and I can do," said Mr. West.

"Nothing except possess our souls in patience," was Warren's reply.

"Do you know, Mr. Warren," West remarked, as he stood in the door of the office before going out, "when I get back to New York I shall serve the same end to all Eastern speculators in California real estate that the drunkard is said to have been used for by old-fashioned temperance lecturers; that is, as a horrible example. Like many another spring lamb, I got excited over the boom and came out here to gather wool; but I'm sorry to say that I shall go back home shorn mighty close; most mighty close," he added, sadly shaking his head.

Warren laughed dubiously and answered,—

"I am even worse off than that. I am shorn, then plucked perfectly smooth, and I fear that I am in danger of losing the hide as well."

"I am sorry to hear it, very sorry," Mr. West replied. "The truth is, that we ought not to have picked up this Oakdale business at all. The boom had burst before ever we touched this matter; blown higher than a kite, in fact. Now, as the result of our fooling with it, we find ourselves lifted with it and filled chock-full of splinters." Then, dropping his voice and looking cautiously around, he asked,—

"Do you suppose Glenn knew all along how things would go?"

"No; Glenn is honest according to his light," Warren answered. "I will answer for his intentions. He is enthusiastic by nature, and he has, before this, made so much money out of this land-craze that he thought it must last forever. As for us, we were green enough to let him talk us out of our seven senses."

"Do you think that the boom will ever pick up again?" West asked, looking very blue.

"That is simply a matter of opinion. If you ask one man, he will tell you 'yes.' If you ask another, he will give you just as positive a 'no.' The truth is, nobody knows anything about it, and we must wait and see."

"I am afraid we are stuck," West remarked, as he nodded his adieu and left the office.

"I'm afraid we are," Warren assented, with a thoroughly dejected air as he seated himself at his desk. Just then, seeing Mitchell pass the door, he went out and called him in.

"Mitchell," he said, as his friend took the seat to which Warren motioned him, "when will you be ready to go on that fishing-trip you promised me?"

"You won't let me off, then?"

"Not a bit of it."

"Then set your own time. If I must be martyred, I will not name the day for my own execution. I draw the line at that," Mitchell replied, with voice and manner expressive of the profoundest resignation.

"What do you say to Monday? Can you be ready?" Warren asked.

"Having no preparations to make, I should think that it would be possible for me to meet that date," Mitchell said.

"All right; Monday it is, then," was Warren's reply.

Mitchell, who had been studying his friend's face carefully during the foregoing conversation, now asked,—

"What is the matter, Warren, if it is not prying into your affairs to inquire? You look positively azure. Has the boom burst?"

"That is just it, Mitchell; and it has carried me aloft in its wake," Warren answered.

Mitchell's face betokened the sympathy the extent of his friend's calamity demanded as he next observed,—

"I don't want to follow the example of Job's immortal friends and say, 'I told you so,' but I am more deeply sorry than I can say to find my worst fears verified. For once you see a prophet who is profoundly grieved at the truthfulness of his predictions. Still, I thought the lots sold well."

"Stool-pigeons, Mitchell; though I give you my word that I never dreamed it until this morning," Warren answered, shortly.

"A-h-h! Paper sales, gotten up by our friend Glenn," Mitchell observed.

Warren nodded assent, then said,—

"We shall either have to raise a round sum by assessment and try to hold over until better times, or else take as much of the tract as we actually own and sow it with barley. As for the rest, if we take this course, since it has never been deeded to us, but we hold it on contract, as we say out here, there is nothing for it but to let the real owners from whom we nominally bought it take the property again."

"Follow the last course; the barley and the forfeit by all means; it will be simply throwing good money after bad to embark anything more in so wild a scheme," was Mitchell's emphatic reply.

"I am of your mind," Warren answered. "Well, I'll go out and interview our guide; make whatever arrangements are necessary for Monday; and then we will see how trout-fishing in the Matilija will act as a counter-irritant for a bursted boom."

CHAPTER XII.

"OH, that this too, too solid flesh would melt instead of turning into a wretched semi-fluid condition and remaining in this nasty sticky state, to my great personal discomfort; or, would that I had the wings of an eagle,—a dove's would hardly answer my purpose. Were this last 'oh' granted, the first would not need to be; and the problem of locomotion would, for me, be forever solved."

As Mitchell uttered this pitiful wail he threw himself upon the ground gasping for breath and bathed in perspiration, fanning himself with his hat the while as vigorously as the feeble energies still remaining in him would permit.

"What ails you, Mitchell? Of all the comrades for roughing it, you are the worst!" Warren answered, half laughing, but altogether impatient, as he stood looking down upon his demoralized friend.

"What ails me? Well, now, that is a question! If you ever attain to my pounds and ounces you will thoroughly appreciate the fact that the problem of rapid, easy, and safe transit is as serious a consideration with overgrown individuals as it is with overgrown cities. But I hope so awful a judgment will never fall upon you." And Mitchell shook his head feebly, with an air of exaggerated solemnity, as he half sat, half lay, under the shade of the great oak where he had first thrown himself.

168

"If you knew that you were going to get done up at nothing you ought not to have come. I dare say I could have found some one else," Warren answered, crossly.

"My boy, free your mind to me to the utmost. I know that tribulation ruffles the temper; and I came along with you partly in a spirit of self-sacrificing friendship: to act as a kind of moral buffer for you to run up against and save you from injury; while I also will be candid and admit that I did come, in part, on selfish grounds, and was in so far influenced by a regard for my own pleasure. For I do enjoy an outing; my heart is still light, even if my body is no longer so," Mitchell replied, assuming his most benignant and paternal manner as he spoke.

Warren gave a grunt expressive of his vexation at the fantastic manner Mitchell had assumed as an offset to his own ill temper; but he made no other answer, his attention being occupied with the wagon which had now come up, laden with provisions and the camping outfit, the horses being driven by the guide.

For an outing in the Matilija Cañon a guide is by no manner of means a necessity. But for two men who know nothing of cooking; and who, furthermore, wish to know nothing either of this or of any other household care, it is pleasant to have some one along to do the disagreeable work, which is just as inevitable in camp life as in home life; while, as neither Mitchell nor Warren were skilled disciples of Izaak Walton, they also felt the need of having some one in the party who would know where to look for the fish, and who would also be able to get them out of the water

H   15

and into the frying-pan when once the spots where they were to be looked for had been found.

The man they had finally pitched upon was an old frontiersman who, in his eventful life, had followed almost every known calling except those belonging to civilization. In his early years he had been a hunter, trapper, and guide. From these callings he had drifted into mining during the days of the gold-craze. Now, in his old age, he lived in a little hut in the outskirts of Ventura, and pretended to cultivate a few acres of land which he had been fortunate enough to buy for a few hundred dollars in the days before the "boom," and, consequently, before land had reached its present inflated valuation. On the strength of his dignity as a land-owner he now claimed the title of rancher for himself. When all the points in his favor and dis-favor had been duly weighed, he was found to be one of those good-natured, thriftless, indolent men who are well known "characters" wherever they live, and who are liked without being respected. In a New England village he would have been a local celebrity, the hanger-on at the grocery, and a recipient of the town's charity. In the genial climate and with the productive soil of California, his land, even under his unskilful and thriftless cultivation, produced enough to keep him in comfort; while his earnings as the general factotum and guide to fishing, camping, and hunting parties gave him a revenue over and above that which he derived from his landed property.

For such expeditions James True was always in de-mand, his fund of anecdotes making him an entertain-ing companion around the camp-fire of an evening;

while no one in the State knew so well as he where
was the best place to go at different seasons of the year;
what one would get if he did go; and—a point, after
all, as important as either of the others—if, after the
places had been shown him, one had not the skill to
find and get the game, Jim could do it for him, while
he was perfectly willing to give his employer all the
credit. Partly owing to his inexhaustible fund of
anecdote, which never lost anything in his telling for
want of brilliant coloring; partly because his name suggested the *sobriquet* by which Bret Harte designated
his most famous character, he was universally known
and spoken of for miles around as "Truthful James."

It was by his advice that Warren and Mitchell had
pitched upon this especial point in the beautiful Matilija
as their camping-ground, and the event showed that
Jim fully deserved his reputation for good taste and
sound judgment in such matters. The cañon, never
wide, had here, owing to a bend in the mountains
which walled it in, widened a little beyond its usual
narrow limits; through the centre of the cañon a creek
ran which was now a mere rill; though when it was
swollen by the winter rains it filled the narrow valley
with a mad torrent.

The crescent-shaped bend where their tent was to be
pitched was floored with firm, soft sand, forming a camp-
ing-site at once clean and pleasant; while they were
also favored with the shade of an oak which would, as
Mitchell said, be their dining-room and parlor, while
the tents would furnish sleeping apartments for all
three of them. No provision for rainy weather was
needed, and this fact makes camp-life a joy in Cali-

fornia; since here one can camp out for months at a
time in the mountains and cañons with no fear that
happiness will be turned into mourning by drenching
storms of rain and wind.

To their left a tiny cascade poured over the towering
cliff, broken into spray before it reached the bottom
of the abyss into which its mimic torrent was poured.
Above, on either side, the mountains reared their crests;
each bush, each leaf, even, on their summits being
distinctly defined against the blue sky-line in the clear
atmosphere.

"Come, Mitchell, aren't you going to help us set
things to rights? You'll have time enough for studying scenery before we break camp," Warren said, as
his friend still lay motionless in the shade.

Without moving in the least; without taking his
eyes from the grandly beautiful scenery by which he
was surrounded, Mitchell answered,—

"Warren, you are but a carnally-minded creature
after all; you have no soulfulness in your soul, or you
would never come thrusting pots and pans, groceries
and bedding, between my eyes and this sublime sight.
Then, you must remember that I am still out of breath,
while I am also sadly weary. No, I am not going to
help you in the least. I shall leave all such grossly
material thoughts and tasks to less sensitively developed minds and less perfectly developed bodies like
yours and Jim's."

Once more Warren growled an answer, for truth
compels us to admit that his losses, both present and
impending, had made him irritable; but Jim now
interposed, saying,—

"Oh, never mind, jedge. Let the pursy gent lie still. Jest help me put up the tent, 'n' then you needn't bother no more. Nothin' like bein' used ter sich work ter shake it off fast."

This proposition was very acceptable to Warren; so, after getting the tent pitched, he left Jim to arrange the rest of the camp equipage according to his own ideas and by his own unaided efforts, unless Mitchell should sufficiently recuperate in his body and relent in his mind as to assist him in the work, which was not at all likely; while he sauntered away to try his luck in fishing, and see if he could be fortunate enough to delude some unhappy trout from the brook with his new rod and patent fly.

After an absence of something more than two hours Warren returned tired and hungry, to find the arrangements for their open-air housekeeping completed and an excellent supper in process of preparation under Jim's skilful management.

Taking off his basket, he laid it on one side, making no reference either to his good or ill success, Mitchell and Jim both watching his movements; the former with an expression on his full and rosy face almost childlike in its innocence; the latter with a meaning smile. Nothing was said about the results of this initiatory fishing expedition, however, and during supper the conversation turned upon entirely different topics. At last, after supper had been despatched and the dishes cleared away, Mitchell remarked, casting an anxious eye towards Warren's basket as he spoke,—

"I say, old man, I think you have left that basket

15*

altogether too near the fire. Those fish will all be
spoiled before morning."

Warren laughed and replied,—

"They'll keep; don't you worry on that score. The
fish I catch always have that peculiar quality of being as
good six months after as they are the day I catch them."

"Fish is dod-gasted queer things, anyhow," Jim
interposed in a meditative tone, now primed and
loaded, and anxious to launch out into one of his
veracious anecdotes, as they sat around the camp-fire
smoking, in the deepening darkness of the evening.
"Leastways some fish is most mighty queer critters,"
he added, in a tone of the profoundest conviction as to
the truth of the statements lying back of these words,
and which had impelled him to speak them.

"Are the fish of this portion of the world peculiar
in their habits above all others? If so, post me,
please, and I will hope for better luck next time I
go after them," Warren said, lighting a cigar; and,
leaning back against the oak-tree, he composed himself
into an easy attitude for listening to the forthcoming tale.

Jim took his pipe from his mouth for the purpose
of overwhelming a "swift," as he designated the lizard
which had indiscreetly ventured within range of his aim,
which had been made fatally accurate by years of long
and painstaking practice. The unhappy reptile lay
perfectly still for a moment, apparently stunned by
the magnitude of the calamity that had overtaken it;
then it scuttled away to the brook in order to repair
damages, if this were possible.

After watching the struggle and flight of his victim
in profound and thoughtful silence, Jim again placed

the stem of his pipe between his lips, drew a few vigorous puffs to make sure that it was well lighted, then launched forth in the attempt to prove to his auditors that his reputation for veracity rested upon good and sufficient grounds.

"I wa'n't speakin' of no fish hereabouts," he answered. "I was talkin' 'bout them air flyin'-fish; bat-fish we usety call 'em back in Kansas."

Warren and Mitchell both roared. "Flying-fish in Kansas!" Mitchell repeated, as soon as he could regain his vocal powers, which had been, for a time, suspended through laughter. "You have succeeded in discovering an entirely new denizen of the prairies, and one hitherto unknown to fame."

"This is a very interesting fact, Jim, and one that ought to be communicated to the world, and not to us alone. If you will give me the county and town in this wonderful State honored by their miraculous presence, I will communicate it to the faculty of natural history at Yale, and you will become immortal, Jim," Warren added.

"'Tain't no miracle, jedge," Jim answered, giving Warren the title his legal profession conferred upon him in the popular estimation. "It's all nateral 'nough. I can't tell you no town they wuz ever in, fer fish don't take ter towns; they do hev schools, though."

"Yes, the scholastic habits of fish are proverbial, I believe; but drive on with your story," Warren replied.

"Wal, 'twuz this way," Jim answered, pressing the tobacco into his pipe with his finger as he spoke.

"I'd bin gittin' hard run fur a right smart spell, 'n' fust I knowed I wuz dead broke 'n' nothin' in my line ter do. 'Twuz down in Kansas, Seward County, 'n' all I could find in my line wuz cattle ranchin', so I hired out on a ranch as a bull-whacker. Wal, the ranch wuz down on the Cimarron River, putty nigh the State line, clus ter the Injun Territory. Feed wuz plenty that year; so the cattle wuz doin' well 'n' lookin' prime, 'n' the boss wuz countin' on big money; but nobody need count on nothin' in that durn kentry.

"'Bout midsummer thar came a big drove o' grass-hoppers, 'n' then we knowed twuz all day with us. Ye never seen sech a sight in yer life. All day, from day-break till sunset, they come, pourin' over the kentry in great swarms. All day long 'twuz like the cloudiest kind o' cloudy weather, with the air full o' snow-flakes bigger 'n yer thumb, if ye can picter ter yerself sech a thing. We had ter keep lights burnin' in the house all day ter see anything; 'n' as fur goin' out, nobody couldn't 'thout an umbrel 'n' gum boots, the air wuz that thick with hoppers, 'n' they wuz piled up on the ground knee-deep on the level."

"It was a kind of a grasshopper-storm, I should say," Mitchell suggested.

"Didn't you need rubber coats when you went out, as well as boots and umbrellas?" Warren asked.

"I don't ask ye ter b'leve me," Jim answered in an injured tone. "I wouldn't swaller no sech darn yarn myself 'f I hadn't seen it; but the toughest part of all is comin' now."

"All right, go on; let us see how much you can give us without choking us," Warren said.

"Wal," Jim resumed, picking up the broken thread of his narrative, "o' course all the cattle died; they starved ter death, for everything was eaten bare,—grass, leaves, 'n' even the bark o' the trees. 'Twuz awful t' hear 'em bellerin' 'n' moanin' as they floundered round in the dark through the hoppers, tryin' ter find suthin' they could eat; but they wa'n't nothin' left.

"The ole man sez at first we'd got ter butcher 'n' pack the meat t' market somehow; but bless yer, who could git round with hoppers knee-deep on the ground 'n' gittin' deeper all the time, 'n' the air full, thicker 'n snow? 'n' the ole man hisself seen that 'n' knocked under.

"'Bout the ninth day, jest for a change, it began ter blow from the south towards evenin', 'n' the hoppers began ter drift, 'n' by mornin' the house wuz putty nigh buried. Then we just felt blue, 'n' don't ye forgit it; it seemed like we wuz shet in ter starve. But while the wind wuz blowin' 'n' the hoppers driftin', afore the howl of the wind 'n' the whir o' the hoppers we could hear a queer rushin' noise, nothin' like what any o' us had ever heard afore. None on us could make out what it wuz, 'n' o' course we couldn't *see*, with the house buried under hoppers.

"Bimeby it seemed like the wind died out, 'n' the hoppers began ter make less noise, like they'd gone on, ye know; but this queer rushin' noise kep' up 'n' growed louder as the other sounds died out 'n' gin it full swing. The next day at sun up they wa'n't a hopper ter be seen; thar the house stood in a clear perary what looked 's if it hed been swep' by fire, 'twuz so bare o' grass; but nary hopper. 'Stead o' them thar wuz the

m

darndest sight enny man ever set eyes on, 'n' one that
jest knocked every man-jack o' us inter a heap.

"The ground wuz kivered 'ith fish,—bat-fish,—
millions on 'em, great big fellers longer 'n yer arm. It
seems they'd scented these hoppers as they flew over
the Cimarron; 'n' these flyin'-fish is mighty fond o'
hoppers, but they can't fly ag'in' the wind. Wal, arter
the hoppers 'd crossed the river, it seems it began
ter blow t'other way, 'n' that wuz what kep' the hoppers
with us so long, 'n' flying-fish, or bat-fish, we called 'em,
couldn't git out o' the river. But when the gale from
the south blowed so hard that it drifted the hoppers,
that wuz jest what the fish wanted; 'n' then the hull
school tuk wing 'n' flew in, 'n' et up every last hopper
on 'em. Thar they lay, stuffed so chock-full 't they
couldn't move, lyin' round on the ground, all but three
or four, what wuz roostin' on the wreck of a tree the
hoppers 'd et most ter a stump."

Jim paused in his narrative and gazed meditatively
into the fire, puffing vigorously at his pipe in the mean
time.

"Well, what became of the fish?" Warren asked.

"We wanted ter let 'em go, seein' the scrape they'd
got us out of; but the ole man wuz a ungrateful old
cuss, 'n' he said no! his cattle wuz all dead; 'n' he
wuz ruined if he couldn't realize off them fish; 'n' if
we wanted him ter stump up ter us when pay-day
came, we'd got ter go in 'n' ketch them fish 'n' butcher
'em; so we did. Came mighty tough, though. Some
on 'em we sent fresh ter Topeka; the rest on 'em we
pickled 'n' sent all over the kentry. Bales on 'em went
East; 'n' I shouldn't wonder ef you gents had seen

some of 'em 'n' like 'nough eat 'em : 'Cimarron Salt
Fish' they wuz marked, called arter the river they
came from, ye know."

"No, I never happened to see any of that brand,"
Warren answered.

Mitchell had said nothing, but sat calmly listening,
his countenance expressing the most implicit confidence
in the story. Now he spoke, saying,—

"How did that little speculation in fish turn out,
Jim?"

"Prime !" that veracious worthy at once replied.
"The boss owned up that he'd done better 'n he'd 'a'
done on the beef. We all reckoned 't he made about
four times what the beef 'd 'a' brought him."

"On what grounds did you base your suspicions to
that effect?" Mitchell asked, with an appearance of
deeply increasing interest.

"Wal, thar wuz sech a right smart o' fish ; 'n' thar
ain't no good fish in Kansas, while some folks over
here in Californy don't keer much fur the fish they hev
here. These fish wuz prime ; I never seen none better,
'n' I've seen mighty good fish in my day ; so he got
his own price, 'n' coined money."

"Warren," Mitchell said, speaking with an air of
profound conviction as to the truth of his own words,
"Warren, here is our chance. We'll petition the Legis-
lature, buy the right to all the flying-fish in Kansas
waters, and get up a great flying-fish trust. There's
millions in it, in the language of the immortal Sellers."

"No use," Jim answered, gravely. "That dodge
won't work. They hain't a bat-fish been seen in
Kansas sence. We all thought that every last fish on

'em come out after the hoppers, 'n' that we wiped 'em
all out; finished up the breed, yer know."

"Too bad!" Warren answered, laughing heartily,
and putting his hand in his pocket as he spoke in
order to take out his watch and look at the time.
"You ought to have sent me after them with a hook
and line; that would have preserved at least a few of
such a valuable and interesting branch of the fish
family as a wonder in the world."

Warren's fingers no sooner reached his watch-pocket
than the smile faded from his face and was replaced by
a look of grave anxiety. He felt in his other pocket,
in all his pockets, but without success; the watch was
certainly gone. This was a loss severely felt by Warren, both because the watch was a valuable one, and
also from the associations connected with it. He rose
to his feet and stood silent, searching his pockets in that
anxious, aimless way which is so prominent a characteristic of perplexed masculine nature, as though it
might, perchance, have been overlooked, and a more
careful search of the pockets would reveal the hidden
treasure lurking in some corner hitherto forgotten.
The darkness concealed his anxious search from his
companions; but Warren soon revealed his loss to
them, and at the same time invoked their sympathy
and aid, saying,—

"Mitchell, Jim, I have lost my watch! Have either
of you seen anything of it?"

"No; *have* you?" Mitchell exclaimed, rising to his
feet with an agility not to be expected in a man of his
weight. "You must have dropped it from your pocket
while you were out fishing."

"True enough! What an ass I was to wear a fob up here among these bushes!" Warren answered, angry at himself for his carelessness, his hands still buried in the pockets of his trousers and turning over their contents in an aimless way.

"We must start out on a hunt for it. Come on, take the lead and show us where you went. Jump up, Jim; your experience is invaluable," said Mitchell.

That worthy, still quietly seated on the ground, was not in the least disturbed by the loss which so profoundly agitated the other members of the party; and so far was he from showing any interest in their distress, even, that he had once more filled his pipe and was occupied in turning over the ashes of the fire, which was now burned out, in search of a live ember to give him a light without unnecessarily consuming his substance by employing a match.

He was too old and experienced an adventurer to waste any thoughts or expend any regrets over losses which are clearly beyond repair, however great they may be; while that philosophy which enables us to endure with unflinching fortitude the disasters of others caused him now to present an unruffled exterior to the present calamity, and one which seemed to Warren and Mitchell, in their distress, the perfection of stoicism.

On being directly addressed, he looked up, replying,—

"'Tain't no manner o' use, gents. They ain't no sense at all in packin' a lantern around among them bushes to-night. Huntin' for a needle in a hay-mow 'd be fun 'long-side o' huntin' for a watch in that chaparral by candle-light. Jest keep quiet 'til mornin'; then we'll stand some show o' findin' it."

16

It was Warren's watch that was lost, not Jim's, and
he could hardly be expected to view the matter in the
calmly philosophic light in which it presented itself to
the experienced eye of the old frontiersman.   He positively refused to postpone the search until morning, a
refusal in which he was supported by Mitchell, while
both insisted that Jim should aid them in the search.
At last he grumblingly assented; the lantern was
lighted, and, Jim taking the lead and "packing" the
light, as he expressed it, they took the route over
which Warren had passed in his fishing excursion of
the afternoon, as nearly as he could point it out, searching the thick chaparral on either side of the trail as
they advanced.

The night was clear and bright, and the moon, just
beginning to rise into view above the mountains, was
riding in pure, cold beauty through the cloudless sky.
On each side of the narrow valley (or cañon, as it is
commonly called) the perpendicular mountains towered,
crowned with here and there an oak-tree, and clothed in
sage-brush, their wrinkled faces forming weird, fantastic
pictures in the moonlight.

Their path lay through the thick, tall chaparral by
the side of the stream which wound its way down
through the cañon; now boiling and rushing over its
rocky bed; now plunging over some boulder in a
mimic water-fall; now madly striking a huge crag,
against which it raged and foamed as though, made
furious with anger at finding its course opposed, it
were striving to overwhelm the barrier raised against
it; then, wearied as well as angered by its fruitless
efforts, without staying in its wild haste, it turned

sharply to the other side of the cañon, to immediately return to its former course when once the crag had been passed. Now calmly and quietly it deepened into broad pools, in whose clear, unrippled surface the moon and stars were mirrored so distinctly that fancy could almost dream that in this wild place the extreme limits of the earth were reached; and now the vast expanse of space lay spread out before human eyes and extended above, below, around them, reaching on into infinity.

Amid scenes of such sublimity and grandeur they pursued their search, and as they paused to rest for a moment beside a pool, Mitchell, as he gazed down into its quiet depths, gave expression to thoughts much like these, saying that it seemed to him almost irreverent and wholly trivial to be searching for a lost watch while you were gazing off into eternity.

As the lost watch was not his property, the weight of the misfortune did not, of course, rest as heavily upon him as it did upon its actual owner; and Warren at once emphatically dissented from any such view of the case, saying that, as it was *his* watch that was lost, he should certainly not suspend the search for sentimental reasons, and that he furthermore proposed to keep it up just as long as there remained the remotest possibility of finding it.

About midnight, however, the search was suspended, and very suddenly at that, for no less a reason than the rebellion of Jim, who flatly and firmly refused to go any farther or spend any more time in the quest that night. He was willing to go on with the search in the morning and hunt until the watch was found,—

or until it was clear that it could never be found; but, for his part, he was through for that night, and remained inflexible in his resolution to go back and "turn in."

Nothing was left for Mitchell and Warren, therefore, but to do the same; and as they retraced their steps Warren anxiously asked him what he thought of the chances of finding the missing property.

"Bless yer heart, thar ain't no manner o' doubt but what ye'll find it. I never knowed it fail but what sech things always turned up sooner or later; 'n' it's mostly sooner," Jim answered.

"Then you have known watches to be lost before?" Warren again asked, determined to press his questions until he found some tangible reasons for hope in his own case.

"Lots on 'em," the truthful guide answered; and now, another veracious reminiscence coming into his mind, he went on,—

"Why, only last year I went out with a party back into the mountains yonder. 'Twuz miles 'n' miles from any suttlemint, 'n' we had ter pack everything over on mules; 'n' when we'd loaded them with all they could carry we had ter pack the rest ourselves. Talk about tired; wal, ruther! When we reached the place whar we wuz ter camp every dad-binged mother's son of us wuz dead beat out, mules 'n' men, with trampin' 'n' scramblin' through the passes, 'n' packin' grub, 'n' guns, 'n' blankets; so, 'thout stoppin' for supper nor nothin' else, we jest unloaded the mules 'n' then lay right down 'n' went ter sleep.

"In the mornin' I wuz waked up by an everlastin' row. Thar wuz a watch missin'. The chap as lost it wuz a Boston feller; a little, finicky, fussy cuss, 'n' he wuz in a terrible takin'. The watch wuz really vallyble, like yourn, sir; 'n' he sot no end o' store by it 'cause 'twuz costly, 'n' 'cause 'twuz handed down to him from way back; wot ye calls a airloom, I b'lievè. Then, he said it kep' time like the sun, 'n' he'd had it put all in fine shape. Now, he said, if he ever found it 'twould be all out o' kilter, 'n' thar wuz no end of a row.

"Wal, all hands started in for a hunt; 'n' at last, down by a crik we'd crossed the day afore, thar it lay, jest the tip o' the stem in the water,—the part ye winds it up by, ye know,—'n' nothin' hurt a bit. I picked it up 'n' handed it to the feller as owned it; 'n' he took it, solemn-like, 'n' looked at it. 'Twuz goin' all right, 'n' it 'd kep' time all right. He tried ter wind it, 'n' 'twuz all wound up tight as it 'd go.

"They wuz all puzzled 'bout this; couldn't see inter it no way 'til I showed 'em how it lay when I found it; then 'twuz all clear. Ye see, jest the tip o' the stem lay in the water; 'n' it lay right with the current; 'n', as the water is powerful swift up in the mountains, it 'd kep' the watch wound up; jest as fast as it run down the current wound it up ag'in. So thar it lay all right; no time lost; nothin' out o' kilter. Wa'n't that Boston chap tickled, though? Oh, no, I reckon not!"

The truthful chronicler of his own adventures now became silent, and nothing was said for some moments, as they picked their way back along the bank of the creek. At last Mitchell called out,—

"Jim, are you sure that watch was not a Waterbury?"

16*

The guide cast a disgusted glance over his shoulder; but, as the sceptic was bringing up the rear of the procession, he failed to see it in the dim light of the night, so it failed to impress him.   Jim thereupon answered,—

"Didn't I tell yer this wuz all back in the mountains?"

"Yes."

"We wa'n't out o' Californy."

"I understand ; but what of that?"

"It's clear ye don't know nothin' about Californy," Jim returned, his voice expressing the deepest compassion for such dense and unenlightened ignorance.

"Not very much ; why?" was Mitchell's reply.

"Why?   Bless yer stup'd noddle, thar ain't water enough in all Californy, if the rivers wuz all turned inter one, ter keep one o' them blamed Waterburys wound up two hours," Jim replied.

Mitchell laughed, but being worn out by his day's exertions, he was too tired to keep up the conversation, so he said no more ; while Warren, for his part, was too thoroughly dispirited to feel any interest in Truthful Jim or his adventures, so the rest of the journey back to camp was accomplished in silence.

With the first break of day Warren resumed his search, leaving his companions still sleeping soundly. At last, far from the camp, and, fortunately for him, far from any of the numerous other parties camping in one part or another of the cañon, Warren found his lost watch, hanging from a bush, suspended by the fob.

With an exclamation of delight he recovered his property and hastily made his way back, to find Mitchell lazily swinging in a hammock reading, while he waited for the breakfast which Jim was busily engaged in preparing.

He was the first to observe Warren's return, and called out to him,—

" What luck ?"

Warren triumphantly held up his watch for a reply, then said,—

" But as I found it hanging on a bush, I was not as lucky as Jim's Boston friend, for my watch has run down. I was in hopes that some twig would brush against the stem enough to keep it wound up, part way at least; but as I had no such luck, will you give me the time, Mitchell ?"

Mitchell complied with the request, while Jim, cutting off a long piece of raw hide, said, as he handed it to Warren, " Here, take off that bit o' fancy tomfoolery, hitch this on, 'n' put it round yer neck. Then ye'll have suthin' on as won't break nor cut easy; then yer watch 'll be safe."

Warren complied with this advice, and then sat down to breakfast with a lighter heart than he had carried before for several days. The clear mountain air, the constant exercise, together with change of occupation and of scene, all combined to divert his mind from his business troubles, while Mitchell, who was always a genial companion, now made especial exertions to entertain his friend and keep him from brooding over his losses. Warren, to his own surprise, found that he was continually becoming more cheerful, while the future, even if it were destined to be one of, to him, comparative poverty, did not seem to him so altogether hopeless as before.

So two weeks passed pleasantly away, when one morning, to the profound astonishment of all but Jim, who was never surprised at whatever might happen, who should march into the camp but Jake Elkins accompanied by a pretty buxom girl, with dark skin and melting black eyes, who leaned affectionately upon his arm, looking up into his face with glances of loving confidence and pride, while he completely paralyzed both Warren and Mitchell, who were already sufficiently overcome with amazement at this sudden apparition, by introducing his companion as Mrs. Elkins, *née* Señorita Camilla Carballo !

CHAPTER XIII.

YES, Jake was actually married. The "settlement" of his difficulties at which he had vaguely hinted some weeks before was not, as Warren had then feared, the wreaking of summary vengeance upon the Carballos, to be accomplished by perpetrating some act of violence upon the person of one of the male members of the family; but he had had in mind all along the intention of solving the problem by the short and easy method of binding Camilla to himself in the silken bonds of matrimony, and leaving their respective parents to overcome their opposition at such a time and through such influences as circumstances should provide.

It was not, however, so easy a matter as Jake had hoped to bring Camilla to view the situation from his stand-point. She was a good girl and a dutiful daughter, and she could not easily be convinced that the mere fact of her being of age released her from the duty of implicit obedience to her father's commands.

Jake had labored industriously to show her that she was not at all obeying the spirit of the divine commandment, nor even the letter of it so perfectly as she supposed; for her father had forbidden her to meet him or even speak to him at all; yet they were continually meeting in defiance of this prohibition; and if she were prepared to disobey in this one point, she would be no more guilty in taking the last step and

189

becoming his wife, while they would be much happier than they now were or ever could be while the present uncomfortable state of affairs continued.

With true feminine want of logic, Camilla failed to be convinced by Jake's reasoning, and could not be made to assent to his views. She was willing to remain his *fiancée* an indefinite length of time in spite of her father's opposition, but she was not ready to become his wife under the same conditions. But the revolution in her feelings which all her lover's eloquence failed to accomplish was, at last, worked by her own affections. She loved Jake with all the passionate ardor of her hot Southern nature; and when, his patience at last being worn out, he assured her that he would no longer consent to occupy a position at once mortifying to himself and absurd in the sight of others; and when, his indignation provoking him into becoming sarcastic, he prophesied that so dutiful a daughter ought to find her days long in the land, and bade her a final good-by,—then it was that the tide of her affections swept away all the marks which had hitherto defined for her the path of her duty, and she declared herself ready to accompany him to the padre at any time that he would set.

Of all the influences which govern our nature, there is none so almost magical in its power as that of pure and ardent love. It works a transformation in character so thorough that, after it has exercised its influence, one cannot tell with any certainty from what the man now is what he has been heretofore.

While it is perfectly true that love never makes the awkward graceful, nor the clumsy fawn-like, neither has it ever been able to endow the ugly with radiant beauty, yet it does bestow a certain dignity upon the man who yields himself to its influence that he did not have before. In his desire to appear attractive in the sight of the woman who is, to him, the best and fairest in all the world, he is stimulated to endeavor to bring to the surface all that there is in himself; and so, under the influence of love, the timid become high-spirited, the weak grow strong, and out of elements which, but for this best and noblest of passions, would have lain dormant forever in the nature of many a man, he develops a new and superior character.

So the Jake who came into the presence of Warren that bright spring morning was a finer-looking and a better man in every way than the one whom he had last seen a few weeks before. But the having attained his object and become possessed of his prize did not, as Jake now found to his surprise and sorrow, bring all his troubles to an end; on the contrary, they were now only well begun, and had he ever heard the words of the old Latin poet—" The rose often lies nearest to the nettles"—he would have set down their author as the wisest of men, one whose incisive genius fell little short of inspiration, in fact; for no sooner had he transplanted the fair flower he had so long coveted to adorn and beautify his own home, than he found that, by doing this, he had caused the nettles and thorns which had hitherto surrounded her, to his vexation, to spring up into a fuller and more dangerous activity, and one which threatened to make his bridal couch a bed of thistles.

But laying aside Ovid's figure and stating the facts

in plain, unmetaphorical language, Jake had counted upon his mother's countenance and support when once he was actually married, and if he possessed this he felt that he could afford to face and defy the opposition of Camilla's family. But he soon found that the solid rock upon which he had hoped to stand was only the veriest sand. No sooner had he introduced his bride to her new mother than this lady gave them to understand, in the unadorned but forcible language upon which she prided herself, that, "having brought up one family, she did not propose to bring up another; and as he had been smart enough to get a wife, he ought to be smart enough to take care of her."

In short, our poor friend's sorrows were only just beginning; and with his bride's family for his mortal enemies, and his own mother a broken reed on whom he could lean only to be pierced, he felt himself friendless at a time when he most needed friends. In this way it came about that his bridal trip resolved itself into a journey to the camp of Warren for the purpose of seeking his countenance and support.

Warren heard his tale of woe without comment. When the narrative was finished he said,—

"Well, Jake, I suppose you see no solution for your present difficulties?"

Jake shook his head dolefully. If he could find one, he would not now be putting himself into the hands of his friend, a thing most repugnant to his newly-awakened manhood, and which made his pride give him many a painful twinge lest, for all her affection for him, his helplessness should lower him in the eyes of his bride.

Warren understood his feelings and sympathized with them. While Jake had, certainly, been unwise in taking to himself a wife when he was not able to provide for himself alone, and then relying upon another to support her, it was too late now to remind him of the fact, so he answered cheerfully,—

"Don't be down-hearted, Jake; there never was a plight so bad that it could not be improved; and now that you think you are in the lowest depths is, I take it, a sure sign that your affairs will take a turn for the better right away. Now take my advice: go down to the hotel below, give yourself no thought of your troubles, but be happy yourself and give your attention to making your wife happy. Neither of you will ever be married but this once,—at least I hope not,—so devote yourself to the honeymoon, and make it as sweet and as brilliant as possible. Meanwhile, I will go down to Ventura and look out for your affairs, and I give you my word that before I come back I will have things arranged in such a shape that you will be better off than you ever were before, and can go back to a home and a business of your own."

After some further conversation, Jake and his bride returned to take rooms in the hotel for their honeymoon, happy and contented in spirit, and feeling that they had not done such a rash and foolish thing after all, and leaving Warren to begin his preparations for a journey back to town.

"Mitchell," he remarked, stropping his razor as he spoke, "does it not seem as though my life was guided by an evil fatality? Here I am now, simply overwhelmed with troubles of my own, when at the very height of my anxiety here comes this boy and adds his share to the general store of misery which I am to look after."

"I don't see any fatality in the matter, my friend," Mitchell replied. "People have an ingenious way of manufacturing trouble for themselves, and then throwing all the responsibility upon Providence. Or else— and I don't know as these grumblers are much more profane than the others—they deny the beneficence of Providence altogether, and swear that they are under a curse. This world and its affairs are, according to them, altogether out of joint; everybody and everything is governed by a relentless and cruel fate; misery and wretchedness only are allotted to mankind, with, perhaps, the exception of a few favored ones; and this all goes to show, beyond the possibility of question, that there is no good and merciful Providence overruling the affairs of men."

"You attribute all human misfortunes to man's own short-sightedness or his own folly, then?" Warren asked.

"Don't you?" Mitchell returned, answering Warren's question by putting another in his turn. Then he went on before his friend could reply:

"I don't want to be guilty of following an I-told-you-so line of argument, but I know of no better illustration of the point under discussion than one which is given me by a certain young friend of my own. This young man came here from the East very recently, wiser than any or all of his friends; he invested pretty much all that he is worth in a visionary scheme; and about the same time he began to play the uncle to a certain young Californian who, having never been brought up to take care of himself, has seen fit to unite his own want of fortune with the equal poverty of a young woman, and then comes to my friend to help him out.

"Now, had this friend of mine, who shall be nameless, been worldly-wise and kept his money in his own hands; and had he been comfortably selfish, and refused to trouble his head with any one's matters except his own, he would not be mourning to-day because his doll is stuffed with sawdust, and bemoaning fate for what is, after all, the outcome of his own doings."

Warren laughed at this graphic review of his recent career, and said,—

"I shall not contradict you, and I do not feel in the mood for pursuing the argument. But, after all, I do not regret anything I have done, the Oakdale investment alone excepted. Jake is a good fellow and well worth all the trouble he makes me; I feel confident that there is good stuff in him, and that he will do well if he can only have half a chance."

"Yes, I like his looks, and I hope you can unearth something for him," Mitchell replied.

"Do you know," Warren resumed, "I find that his troubles are proving an excellent counterpoise to my own calamities. I think it must be that there is a spice of the savage in us all; for, as Lucretius found such solid satisfaction in standing on the shore and watching a ship founder out on the sea, because the wretchedness of the unfortunate sailors contrasted so comfortably with his own security, I find that I am beginning to feel quite cheerful since Jake has interviewed me;

though I hope that the feeling grows out of the nobler sentiment of liking the young man and wishing to help him, rather than out of the heathenish satisfaction one finds in seeing somebody worse off than himself."

"Who dare vouch for his own motives?" Mitchell replied. "Cheer up, my friend, so far as this case is concerned, for I am certain that in this instance at least the nobler motive prevails with you. I feel confident of this for two reasons: First, I draw my firm conviction of this from grounds derived from a long and careful contemplation of your character; secondly, because I am far from certain that the young fellow is worse off than yourself. You are sure to find some means of helping him out of his scrape; and 'if siller 'll dae it,' as the Scotchman said, you may draw on me for any reasonable amount; I'll commit the decision as to what a reasonable amount is to your judgment and also to your conscience. In your own case, however, the ditch into which the ass has plunged headforemost is so exceedingly deep and wide, I doubt if you will find any one daring enough to stretch out a helping hand."

"I thank you, Mitchell, both for your generosity to Jake and your highly complimentary reference to myself," Warren answered.

All preparations being now made, Warren took his departure from the camp and set out upon his philanthropic errand, leaving Mitchell, as he expressed it, to keep Jim in good nature and the house in good order until he could return.

As he could not arrive in Ventura before nightfall, his peace-making errands were, perforce, deferred until the next day ; and as he regarded Mrs. Elkins as the more difficult as well as the more uncomfortable to manage of the two parties whom he had come to visit, he did not wish to call upon her until he had learned how his mission would be received by Carballo, when he would be able to meet her with some preconceived plan of action in his mind, and have the strategic advantage altogether with himself. As it would serve no good end to meet her at all until he did so for the purpose of definitely discussing Jake's prospects and ascertaining positively what she would, or would not, do for him, instead of going to his rooms at her house, he went at once to the Hôtel Anacapa on reaching town.

The next morning, without incurring any unnecessary loss of time,. Warren went out to do the work and (if such a thing were possible of accomplishment) to earn for himself the blessing of the peace-maker.

It was a task for which he had no relish, and in the performance of which he was well aware there would be no pleasure. He thoroughly appreciated its delicacy, and, fully realizing the truth of the proverb, "it is seldom safe to instruct even our friends," he foresaw the difficulty of avoiding the giving of offence when he attempted to advise the proud old Spaniard as to the conduct he ought to pursue towards the daughter who had so bitterly displeased him in her choice of a husband.

If, however, it were possible to bring about a reconciliation, Warren was peculiarly well fitted for effecting it. He was a genial and whole-souled young man, pleasant in his manners, and he knew, no one better, how to ply his arguments in a pleasant way which would, at the same time, cause them to carry conviction to the mind of the listener from the address with which they were put.

Laying aside all thought of his distaste for the task, he dismounted before Carballo's gate to make his first essay in behalf of his friend.

The place was on the outskirts of the rural city, and the house was a quaint combination of the past and the present, in perfect harmony with the character of its inhabitants. The main portion of the building was adobe, the thick walls having been surfaced and painted white; the old tiled roof of ancient days had, however, disappeared, giving place to modern shingles; and although this innovation had caused the house to lose in its romantic effect, the loss was more than compensated in the estimation of its denizens by the added comfort the change had brought to them.

The needs of the family had long outgrown the proportions of the original edifice, so wings had been added from time to time; these additions had, however, been built of wood, and, like the main building, had been painted white; and the general result had been a long, low, rambling structure, part adobe, part wood, quaint in its appearance, and pleasing from its very quaintness.

The house was shaded by a huge fig-tree, while at one side an almond was waving its feathery leaves in the soft and fragrant breeze. The yard was filled with roses and other flowering shrubs, while the porch was buried beneath a huge passion-vine. Back of the house was a thrifty walnut-orchard, while the whole appearance of the place showed that it was the home of one fairly prosperous, if not possessed of absolute wealth.

Warren knocked at the door, which was immediately opened by an elderly man, who bade him enter with the polite courtesy inherited from his Spanish ancestors, and cherished with the proud tenacity of devotion with which the Spanish-Americans of pure blood and good birth cling to all the traditions and customs of their old Castilian home.

"Señor Carballo, I believe?" said Warren, entering the house in response to the invitation.

"The same," was the reply.

"My name is Warren, and I will say at once that no one knows better than myself the delicacy of the business upon which I have called."

The old gentleman bowed, but made no other response, although the serious expression that his countenance assumed upon hearing this showed his visitor that he at least suspected the causes which had brought about the doubtful pleasure of this call. Warren, seeing that he was compelled to assume the initiative, plunged at once into the midst of the matter, saying,—

"There is a young man in this place for whom I entertain very friendly feelings, and it is with the deepest regret that I learn that he has behaved in a very unhandsome manner towards you."

The best of men are weak. Their greatest strength is only profound weakness, after all; and fond as we are of Warren, and as much as we admire him in the main, we cannot altogether acquit him of the charge of slight duplicity in the present instance. His previous conversations with Jake, and the advice he had then

given him, could have only one tendency, and that
was to bring about this. very method of procedure
which his *protégé* had at last adopted, and which he
was now describing as unhandsome behavior. In his
heart he was at this very moment approving of what
Jake had done, in so far as the act itself was concerned, and he charged him in his own mind with
nothing worse than precipitancy in marrying the girl
before he was so situated that he could take care of
her himself. Yet there he sat, calmly talking to
Jake's father-in-law about the young man's unhandsome behavior, when he had only done what Warren
himself would have done under similar circumstances,
and as he had already as good as advised him to do.

Warren certainly was not ingenuous in this, and we
can only pardon him when we remember how often
we all of us fail in this same respect; when we also
take into consideration what an unendurable place this
world would be were we all of us at all times perfectly
frank and outspoken, and when we reflect upon the
ruinous havoc it would work in our manners and
morals did we all of us say, on all occasions, without
any manner of disguise whatever, exactly what we
think, and try to show, without any attempt at soften-
ing the truth, exactly what we believe.

The old Spaniard's face darkened and became almost
savage in its expression as he replied,—

"Ah, you mean young Elkins; he is a villain! he
is an unmitigated scoundrel, whom I would rejoice to
sweep from off the face of the earth as a reptile who
defiles it by his presence. If you call him a friend, I
fear that your friends are not always well chosen, señor."

Warren paid no attention to this severe snub, but answered in his pleasantest tone and manner :

" I regret most deeply the pain his indiscretion has caused you ; and I assure you that you have my deepest sympathy in this great sorrow. My acquaintance with him is, of course, of the briefest, and consequently my knowledge of his character is only superficial. The language you have used in reference to him seems to me intended to warn me that there is something in his past life of which I am still in ignorance that is not altogether to his credit. I should be most grateful to you if you would admit me into your confidence so far as to justify your bad opinion of the young man to me ; for, of course, I should be most unwilling to befriend any one who is thoroughly unworthy or who has shown himself a villain. I, on my part, will be equally open with you, and will admit that I had formed the best opinion of the young fellow's character and principles."

With these words Warren leaned over towards his host, the expression on his face being that of one who was expecting to listen to a tale of the most harrowing enormities which would fall little, if at all, short of proving actual crimes, and who was prepared to sift to the bottom with a calm and judicial mind all the evidence, *pro* and *con*, now to be laid before him.

Señor Carballo was evidently staggered for a moment. This method of approaching the subject was altogether unfamiliar to him, and it was foreign to the fiery temper and hot prejudices of his ardent and impetuous race. He hesitated for an instant, and then, without directly answering Warren's question, he proceeded to deal with the case from his own stand-point.

"Is not his treatment of me, señor, the conduct of a villain?" he sternly demanded. "Has he not crept into this family nest like a slimy, poisonous serpent, and stolen from it the fairest of the brood? I have nothing further to say; and it seems very clear to me that there is no room here for more words."

"Ah, señor," Warren answered, his voice pathetic with a sympathy that was not now assumed, for no one could see the old man's evident suffering without feeling deeply for him,—"ah, señor, I understand something of your feelings, and believe me when I tell you that I sympathize deeply with you. But there is another side to this, as to all other questions; and bear with me when I say that perhaps I, being altogether a disinterested party, can here see the truth more clearly than yourself. For you know that where we are ourselves deeply interested, we always feel keenly, and so are not prepared to see anything except as our own feelings and prejudices color it."

"Say nothing to me about that wretch, señor, I will hear nothing of him," Carballo angrily interposed.

Warren at once made haste to calm his anger by replying,—

"You mistake my meaning, for I did not intend to present his case, but that of your daughter. She is a lovely girl, whom I both know and admire, and I can readily believe that she merits the graceful name you have given her in calling her the fairest of the home brood.

"Now, you must remember, señor, that she has met

a young man of good family, fair present prospects, and who is also, as you admit, beyond reproach in his character. These two young people became devotedly in love with one another; and where there is perfect love between two young people, with no objection which can reasonably be raised against either one of them, and, moreover, when the young man can offer the lady of his choice a life of comfort, and even the enjoyment of wealth, is their marriage a wrong?"

"It is, by the saints! for I forbade my daughter even to think of him," Carballo replied, fury in his tone and on his face.

Jake's father-in-law was unreasonable, beyond any question, and it was a sore trial to Warren's patience to deal with him; but nothing would be gained were he also to lose temper, while any betrayal of ruffled spirits on his part would only increase the anger of his hot-tempered companion and spoil everything. So, restraining his impatience by an effort, Warren once more applied himself to the task before him, saying,—

"So many years have not as yet rolled over your own head that you should have altogether forgotten the days of your courtship." (The old man was seventy if he was a day.)

"When people are in love they cannot keep their thoughts under control, and they cannot think and feel as their parents command. You should make allowance accordingly, señor."

His host was softened towards him slightly by the reference to his youthful appearance; and, smiling a very little, he abruptly asked,—

"Are you a married man?"

"No," Warren replied.

"But you must be 'engaged,' then, as you Americans say?" Carballo insisted.

Warren blushed slightly as he answered, "No, I am not even 'engaged,'" at the same time hoping that the old gentleman would press his inquiries no further.

This mercy was shown him, Carballo merely saying, in reply to Warren's last answer,—

"Pardon me, but I thought so ardent and so eloquent an advocate of the 'tender passion'—I believe that is your American phrase, is it not?—must have had an experience in it himself, and would at least prove to be a lover. Go on, you interest me."

Warren winced at this home thrust, but returned no answer; he blushed deeply, however, as he resumed his argument, saying,—

"You must remember, señor, that your daughter's happiness depends upon your action. Had she, in the first place, listened to you and dismissed her lover, this would have affected her whole future. If you now persist in refusing to receive her into favor again, you cause her a life-long unhappiness. Had she married unworthily, the whole affair would, of course, wear a different aspect and my arguments would be worthless; but since you yourself admit that your daughter's husband is a worthy young man, and that your objection to him rests only upon the simple fact that you personally dislike him, can you hope to confidently face your Maker at the last day, and say that you have faithfully fulfilled your duties as a parent, if you persist in your present mind?"

Like all high-caste Spaniards, Carballo was profoundly influenced by his religious instincts, and this
appeal to conscience and religion accomplished more
for Warren in effecting the reconciliation he was endeavoring to bring about than had been done by all
the arguments he had hitherto employed; and seeing
by the changing expression on the old gentleman's face
the weight his last words had carried with them, he at
once pressed his point warmly.

"I am not alone in my opinion, señor," he resumed.
"Had not the padre looked upon the case in the same
light in which I view it, do you think that he would
have married them without your consent?"

"Ah, he was too hasty, he was too hasty. In that
he did me great wrong," Carballo answered, rising and
walking up and down the room. Then, stopping in
front of Warren, he said,—

"You would have me take in these two young fools
and support them, I doubt not. My fascinating son-
in-law has no means of his own; and you would have
me care for them and their children, if they have them,
until the course of nature causes him to inherit his
mother's fortune. I have stated your idea, have I not?"

Carballo's tone was bitter enough, certainly, and his
manner was far removed from Warren's idea of a pro-
pitiated bearing; but he felt that the old man had
sufficient cause to feel aggrieved, and it was only natural that some of his anger should fall upon a visitor
who confessed that he was a friend and partisan of the
young runaways, and who acknowledged that he had
called for no other purpose than to espouse their cause
and plead for their forgiveness.

Then, a sense of personal responsibility for Jake's conduct made him feel as though he were to a certain extent an abettor of his wrong-doing; and that whatever annoyance he was now experiencing descended upon a head not altogether free from guilt as a well-merited punishment. So, without answering either the spirit or the word of Carballo's question, he proceeded to frankly explain his ideas as to the future of the young couple.

"No," he began, "I do not think that either you or any one else should support them. Jake should be able to care for his own wife and family, if he have one, and you will find that he will do so. There is a nice ranch down by the Santa Clara River,—the Potter place, you know it. His mother will give this to him as a wedding-present; so you need feel no anxiety as to his future. If this is all that is causing you uneasiness, you may lay aside both your anger and your alarm."

Carballo turned suddenly towards his guest with a gesture of amazement and incredulity upon hearing these words.

"You say that this young man's mother will give him the Potter place?"

"I do."

"Pardon me, señor, but she has not the reputation for so great generosity. Will you tell me your grounds for this belief?"

This Warren by no means felt ready to do. In fact, as his assertion was based upon his own powers of persuasion and influence with the lady, he felt that it would be altogether premature to make any further revelations. But in case he should fail in this quarter, as he was prepared to make good his words at his own expense together with the offer Mitchell had made him in Jake's behalf, he did not recede a particle from the position he had taken.

"Pardon me, señor, but I am not at liberty to say more at present," he replied. "But believe me, I know what I say when I assure you that inside of forty-eight hours from now the deeds will be drawn and recorded,—unless you interfere to prevent it; and it would give me great pleasure to take back to the bride the message of her father's affection and forgiveness as well as the title to her new home."

The old gentleman paced back and forth through the room for several moments, wrapped in the deepest thought. At last he once more stopped before Warren, and, looking sharply in his face, he said,—

"If your words are made good, and I find that Elkins does become the owner of this ranch, my daughter and her husband shall be welcome to my house. You may assure her of this, but be sure that you remember the terms. As for him, I do not promise him the love of a father, but he will be courteously received whenever he may choose to come."

Warren rose, and after assuring the old man of the pleasure it would be to him to carry to his daughter this pledge of reconciliation, he took his leave.

"Well, I have gotten so much off my hands," he said to himself as he mounted his horse. "Now for Mother Elkins, and I hardly know whether to think that the worst or the easiest part of this business is now before me."

He found that estimable lady, as usual, overwhelmed with cares and driven almost to her death by the work which, for some reason, never was accomplished, and which every one except herself well knew never would be.

"Bless me, Mr. Warren, where did you drop from? I didn't expect to see you again for six weeks at least," she exclaimed, as he entered the house. Seating himself on the lounge he pointed to a chair, saying,—

"Sit down, Mother Elkins, I want to talk to you."

"Mother Elkins, indeed! What do you mean by talking to me in that style?" she exclaimed, complying with his request at the same time.

"I mean that you'll have to adopt me in the place of that scapegrace boy of your own. And, by the way, speaking of him, I saw him and his bride yesterday. What a right pretty girl she is, isn't she? I wish I could have got in ahead of him. Do you know her well?"

The flax was now all in a flame.

"Know her! I should say I did! The brazen little baggage! I wish I could give her the trouncing she deserves."

This was what Warren had expected; and, to tell the truth, he had intended to bring about this, or some similar outbreak. Now he determined to make short work of the business and he went to the pith of the matter at once.

"See here, Mrs. Elkins," he said, very quietly but none the less emphatically. "I know you, and for that reason I know that your bark is a good deal worse than your bite. As for Jake's marriage, the thing is done now and over with; so it is in very bad taste for you to make all this fuss about it; and the sooner you realize that your scolding won't affect matters the least in the world, the happier you will be. Now, keep your temper while I tell you just what I think.

"My candid opinion now, and so it has been all along, is that you and Carballo have been very foolish about this love-affair. You can't keep up race prejudices in this country; our institutions and customs all prevent it. You are both of you Americans, and the fact that your great-grandfather came from England and his from Spain don't make either one of you the less American, and the younger generation will find this out even if you are too obstinate to do so. Now, all you can do is to make the best of this fact; and I am going right on from this text to give you a little more plain talk which it won't do you the least good in the world to get cross over.

"You haven't done right by the boy; you haven't brought him up properly; you should have had him earn his own living, and you should have taught him to be a man, and like other men to become manly. I have felt this strongly ever since I first knew him, and I have been all along trying to find an opening for him, which I should have done before this had I not had bad luck myself. But that is neither here nor there: if you had only done your duty by him he would have turned out a fine, manly young fellow, instead of growing up the great hobbledehoy he is."

Mrs. Elkins did not heed his warning, and, use or no use, she became very angry with him. No mother relishes being told that she has failed to do her duty by her children. Neither, even though she is angry with them herself, does she enjoy hearing other people criticise them or call them names; while it is especially galling to the mother of an only son, whom she devotedly loves and of whom she is excessively proud, to hear him designated by so uncomplimentary an epithet as hobbledehoy. Mrs. Elkins accordingly waxed exceeding wroth at Warren's language and proceeded to unbosom herself at once.

"Upon my word, Mr. Warren, you are extremely polite this morning," she exclaimed, hotly. "And I never in my life saw an old bachelor, or an old maid either, for that matter, who didn't have the whole science of bringing up other people's children at their tongue's end. I'm sure it's a thousand pities that you are not married, and I hope you will be before long, and that you will have a dozen children, too, whom you can hold up as models for the world to profit by. It will be a misfortune beyond repair if such an example of paternal wisdom as you give promise of becoming is lost to the world."

Warren laughed heartily at this outburst of temper. He had been hoping that he might succeed in bringing down her wrath upon his own head, as being the surest means of dispelling the cloud of disfavor at present overshadowing Jake and his bride. Having gained his point in this respect, he now lost no time in bringing matters to a crisis.

"Gently, gently," he answered. "I told you in the first place that there was no manner of use in your losing your temper with me, and you forget my warning as soon as I have given it. Now let us discuss this business in a reasonable way and like reasonable beings. I have just come from Carballo's."

"You have, have you? Well, what does the old Greaser say for himself?" she asked, spitefully.

"Now don't let your angry passions rise again, and, above all things, don't call names; that is shockingly weak," Warren answered, with aggravating calmness. "I found him a very estimable, a very polite, and, I can truthfully add, a very polished gentleman. As for what he said, he was angry about the elopement, of course; but I found him amenable to reason, and he promised me that he would forgive the young runaways, and that he would take Jake into favor. He would not promise to love him as a son all at once, neither was I able to induce him to consent to bestow upon him the affection of a brother, even, as yet; but we must not expect too much at first; it will all come right in time."

Mrs. Elkins looked very much surprised at this news, and it must be confessed that she did not seem to be altogether rejoiced at hearing it. Her own opposition to the match had been provoked in the first place by the hostility of Carballo, and it had by this time become almost a point of conscience with her to regard the family as "foreigners," and to look upon them as being, for that reason, altogether beneath contempt; and now to be told that everything was smooth in this quarter, and that she alone was playing the part of the cruel parent, was certainly a heavy blow; for no one enjoys finding a cherished grievance demolished so effectually and so altogether without warning.

She returned no answer, however, but only replied by a grunt which she meant to be expressive of the deepest indignation and contempt.

"To equal his good-natured complacency, I made a promise in your name," Warren added.

"Oh, you did, did you? I'm sure I ought to be much obliged for your thoughtfulness; but I ain't, all the same. What promise did you so kindly make in my name?"

"I promised, in the first place, that you would be as considerate to the young people as he had shown himself. Then, in the second place, as I saw that the old gentleman seemed very anxious about the support of these two young people, I told him that you would see that they were made able to take care of themselves, and that you would give Jake as his own property that fine ranch known as the Potter place," Warren answered, in his blandest tone and most insinuating manner.

It was well for him that he did not hold his landlady or her tongue in the least fear, for her anger now blazed forth and burned hotly against him.

"Well, I'm sure!" she exclaimed, fairly gasping for breath in her surprise and anger. "Of all the cool assurance I ever knew, and you less than six months ago a perfect stranger! I have as good a mind as ever I had to do anything to turn you out of my house on to the sidewalk and throw your traps after you, and never let you darken my doors again. The idea of your daring to promise away thousands of dollars in that style right out of my pocket! Did any one ever hear of such brazen assurance! Of course you are not crazy enough to expect me to make such a promise good?"

"Eight thousand dollars is what I pledged you for," Warren replied, as sweetly as before, not in the least moved by her anger. "I happen to know the price to a cent, as the property is in our hands for sale. As to making my words good, that is for you to decide; I can't answer that question for you. It is only right, fair, and just to Jake that he should have a start in life and be given a fair chance for making his own way in the world. As you can well afford to do this for him, I had no scruples about making a promise in your name that you would deal justly by your own son. If, however, you do not feel disposed to act in this manner towards him, Jake shall not suffer in any case; for my friend Mr. Mitchell has promised me that he will join me in purchasing the place for him, and we will let him pay us back by instalments as he is able. You see that we believe in him, even if you don't," he added, as he rose to go.

"Don't fly off in that style," she answered; "sit down and give a body a chance to think, can't you?"

Warren laughed as he complied with her request, not forgetting to remind her that she was the one who had done all the flying.

"Well," she said, after some further discussion, during which she had been driven from one defence to another, all of which she had adopted so as not to appear to yield too readily, "you and that Mr. Mitchell, there, have got me into a corner, and you knew all along that you could do anything you chose

with me; for of course I cannot have folks saying
that I was so stingy that I let strangers take care
of my son rather than do it myself. Go down to
your office and draw up the deeds, and I will give
you a check for the money when you bring them up
to me."

Warren thanked her in the name of Jake and his
bride, congratulated her upon the possession of so
pretty and lovable a daughter, and left her restored
to good nature, while he went down to his office with
the comfortable feeling that he had performed a good
deed in a very good manner.

He pictured to himself the delight with which his
protégés would receive the news that peace was at last
established between the two families now so closely and
intimately connected. He could already, in imagination, see Camilla's bright eyes sparkle with increased
brilliancy at the news that now she was the mistress
of a pretty home of her own. But it is, for some wise
reason, ordained that no one shall know a long con-
tinuance of untroubled happiness in this world, and
Warren's pleasant emotions were, on this occasion, exceedingly short-lived. Perhaps it might have been so
ordered to prevent the growth of self-satisfaction in his
spirit; perhaps it was for some other reason; but be
this as it may, his comfortable feelings lasted only the
few moments required to ride from Mrs. Elkins's house
to his office, where he found Glenn, who greeted him
with,—

"Glad to see you, Warren; I was just going to send
up after you. It's lucky you are down. Come in
here."

Together they disappeared within the mysterious precincts of their private office, from which Warren emerged in half an hour with a very anxious face, for the purpose of writing a note which he forthwith forwarded to Mitchell, informing him that he was detained by business and could not return to camp in less than a fortnight at the shortest limit.

CHAPTER XIV.

THE change in Warren's plans brought about by the imperious demands of business produced a general readjustment of existing arrangements in our little circle of friends.

The note which he despatched to Mitchell, informing him of the inevitable postponement of his return for a fortnight at least, was received by that worthy individual in his characteristic manner. The rule by which he guided his life was, to permit nothing to ever disturb him in the least; and acting always in strict accordance with this rule, he would permit nothing less than a cataclysm in his domestic affairs, or an entire revolution in mundane matters, at least in so far as the last of these affected him, to either hasten his goings or delay his comings one hour from the time he had originally planned.

When Warren's note reached him he was not disturbed in any way, not even put out; but, calmly sitting down, he wrote at once to his wife, requesting that she and Mollie join him in the Matilija. He told them that the baby need be no impediment, for the nurse could come with them; and then if, on trial, camping with a baby should prove to have drawbacks too great to be overcome, the hotel was not a great distance from them, and they could transfer their headquarters to that. As for himself, he said that he had no intention at all of returning under the six weeks for which he had originally set out; but he found it far from pleasant up there in the cañon all alone, and he besought them to have mercy on him in his present widowed and orphaned condition, and to come to his relief.

At the same time that he sent this letter to his wife he despatched Jim to provide another tent and camping outfit for the ladies, in order that they might find everything ready for them on their arrival.

This characteristic letter was received with great merriment by Mrs. Mitchell and her sister, but they consented at once to meet the wishes of its writer. Mollie decided that it would be "great fun," and pretended to feel very much aggrieved because they had not been included in the party in the first place, and were now made welcome only as a last resort. Mrs. Mitchell by no means looked upon the expedition with such favor. She had been long enough now in California to know that, being summer, as there would be no rain, there could be no exposure; still, with a child to care for, she preferred more elaborate housekeeping arrangements than would be possible for her with two tents and an oak-tree for her domicile. She yielded her own wishes, however, to those of her husband and her sister, simply saying that as she consented to the plan to please them, they must share with her the care of the child and all the trouble that he might cause.

The first week passed merrily and pleasantly away. Early in the second week a letter came from Warren, which Jim handed to Mitchell while they were still seated at dinner, in which he told his friend the news

K   19

of himself and his affairs up to date, and informing him that he should return the next day. He took pains, however, to assure them that his advent need cause no disturbance in the little family party which had so happily gathered under the oak since his departure, as he, for his part, would be most heartily glad to welcome the ladies, and pledging his honor as a bachelor that he would bear without a murmur any disturbance that his namesake might create.

But in spite of all his efforts to appear cheerful, it was far from reading like a happy letter. It is hard for a man, after witnessing the downfall of his fortunes, to be possessed of high spirits, or to put his thoughts on paper in such a way that his correspondent will be induced to believe that he has written in a joyous mood. The attempt is as natural, and it results in as close an imitation of reality, as the cheerfulness which the Roman emperors and their estimable modern imitators, the French revolutionists, compelled the families of their victims to assume as good citizens, because their domestic bereavement had resulted in the welfare of the state. Mitchell read his letter to the end with a countenance unusually sober. After finishing it he looked up, still holding it open before him, saying,—

"Girls, this is from Warren. He will be with us to-morrow."

Mollie looked down at her plate and said nothing. Mrs. Mitchell, however, answered at once, and rather sharply, "We have received decidedly short notice, for of course he will want us and the child away."

"Not at all. He could hardly ask that, knowing that I sent for you after he had abandoned me; and he tells me to urge you to stay in case you should express any intention of leaving. I know that he is sincere in this, for the tone of the poor fellow's letter shows very plainly that he is in need of the sympathy of cheerful and congenial friends."

Mollie was still silent, but she looked up quickly at this, her features showing how profoundly interested she was in the conversation, while they also told that she was disposed to be one of the sympathetic friends of whom her brother-in-law had said his friend was now so sorely in need ; and again her sister was the only one who made reply, and this time, noticing her husband's serious expression, she became impressed by the fact that something more than usually serious must be the matter ; and, in expectation of hearing bad news, she asked, anxiously,—

" What does he say? I hope there is nothing wrong with him."

" I am sorry to say that things are altogether wrong with him ; and although nothing has happened beyond what I have been expecting all along, yet I feel just as sorry for him now that the blow has actually fallen as though it had been wholly unexpected. That Oakdale business has fallen flat at last ; and although he doesn't say much about it, it is what he fails to say that impresses me."

The Oakdale boom had burst; such was the unhappy truth. And, as you have undoubtedly suspected all along, this unfortunate failure of the Oakdale Land and Water Company was the business which had detained Warren so long in town busily engaged in the attempt to save as much as possible of the money embarked in this rash and unfortunate speculation.

The "boom" was dead throughout the whole of Southern California, and it was already in its death-throes when the scheme was first floated, had its projectors only known it; or, rather, had they only been frank enough with themselves and others to recognize the fact and admit it. With the collapse of this speculative mania, which passed away as suddenly as it had come, all call for such property as the Oakdale Company placed on the market (which was at the best nothing but lots in a mushroom town, where no one wanted to build, and which were bought with no idea of building on them on the part of the purchasers) had also passed away. There was no present market; there was no prospect of selling more lots than had already been disposed of either in the near or remote future. Whether there would ever again be an opportunity of disposing of this property was more than any man could tell.

Meanwhile, it was a tremendous expense to the little company to hold the tract, for it had been bought by them during the wildest days of the great land-craze at the high figures which all real estate then reached, and at which they were held for a short period. Only a portion of the tract had been wholly paid for, the remainder being bought on credit in the hope that speedy sales of town lots at "boom" prices would enable them to pay all indebtedness on the land, together with the expense of its improvement, and at the same time leave them a handsome profit.

This hope the failure of the Great Oakdale Land

Sale had proved to be fallacious. The expiration of the time for meeting the last payment, coming so soon after this disastrous auction, brought the company face to face with the problem, What is now to be done? Shall the company fail to meet this payment, forfeit the portion of the tract held on contract, sacrificing the payments already made as well as the money expended in improvements, or, would it be wiser for them to raise the money needed to complete the payment and hold the entire tract?

In one way or another these questions must be answered, and at once. Glenn was anxious that the company should adopt some plan for raising the round sum still needed for completing the payment, and that the tract should be held for the brighter times which he prophesied would shortly dawn for them. His partners were also anxious to retain the property, if it were possible, for no one likes to sacrifice his money and see it go from him bringing no return; while the worst sensation of all is the chilling knowledge that he has deliberately thrown away some thousands of dollars. But the raising of the necessary amount was in itself a difficulty which gave promise, from the first suggestion of the idea, of being insuperable.

Two courses were possible of adoption, and only two. The one was, to increase the company by taking in new stockholders; the other was, to assess the present stockholders an amount sufficient to clear off all indebtedness on the property, together with the interest, which had now become due.

The first of these plans was at once dismissed, for no one could be found who would embark his money in a scheme which was universally considered a losing investment. The second was impracticable, for all the stockholders, with the single exception of Glenn, who had no money to invest, positively refused to risk another dollar in the enterprise. Much as they regretted losing their money, they all agreed that it was better to let go what was already at stake than to increase losses which were already heavy; while Warren declared that, for his part, as he had already brought himself to the verge of ruin, he did not propose to go on and complete the destruction of his fortunes by stripping himself of the little he now had left.

It was at the close of this meeting, which had finally decided the fate of the Oakdale Company, and whose action had conclusively determined that Oakdale, notwithstanding the brilliant future which the gifted auctioneer from Los Angeles had predicted for it, was never to be numbered among the actually existing towns of California, that Warren wrote to Mitchell to inform him of the downfall of this great air-castle, whose collapse, with the various causes which finally compassed its destruction, Mitchell explained to the ladies at even greater length than they have been inflicted upon the reader.

"I hope this failure has not ruined him," Mrs. Mitchell remarked, after the usual feminine inquiries as to the reason why all these different steps and various transactions were necessary had been made and answered to her satisfaction.

"That depends altogether upon what you mean by 'ruined,'" Mitchell answered. "He won't have to go out and work by the day exactly, but he has been hit pretty hard for all that."

"What a silly thing it was for him to go in with that dreadful Glenn!" she answered, in a meditative tone; then, drawing a sigh of satisfaction, as the comfortable thought crossed her mind that she was blessed with a husband too wise to ever be led into that most unsubstantial and unsatisfactory of all the departments of architecture known as the building of castles in Spain (though I could never see why they were so called; for surely those feudal structures would be quite as profitable an investment in that country as in any other), she added,—

"How thankful I am, John, that you did not let Mr. Warren influence you into investing in this company!"

"Humph! I haven't quite taken leave of my senses; and if he had been anything better than an unmitigated ass, he would have kept out of any such speculation as that himself," Mitchell answered, contemptuously.

Mollie now spoke for the first time since Warren's affairs had been mentioned; taking fire at her brother-in-law's contemptuous allusion to his friend, she answered, severely,—

"I don't think that was at all nice of you, John Addison. I think it very bad taste in you to sit here and call your friend harsh names behind his back. I remember when you reproved me not so very long ago for speaking ill of him; and I am sure I never called him a fool. I would think I hurt myself more than any one else if I were to call my worst enemy that; and I certainly would *scorn* to say such things of a

friend," throwing an emphasis expressive of the deepest
of righteous indignation upon the last words.

Mitchell gave a long whistle indicative of extreme
surprise upon receiving this rebuke from so wholly
unexpected a source.

"Crushed again," he answered, with an assumption
of extreme contrition. "What has converted you all
of a sudden into so warm a partisan and advocate of
our speculative friend?"

"I am neither a partisan nor an advocate of Mr.
Warren, or of any one else, for that matter, and I don't
like you to call me so even in jest," she replied; "but
when I see so plainly as I did a moment ago that you
are both unjust and unkind I shall certainly be a true
enough friend to you to tell you of it; and I am sure
that you would not wish me to be selfish enough to
keep silence while you abuse your friends."

In common with the rest of his sex, Mitchell looked
upon the female portion of his family as fair game on
which to perpetrate his practical jokes and vent his
witticisms; and it was his especial delight to involve
either his wife or Mollie in a discussion, and then,
after reducing them to silence by his sophistries, laugh
at their indignant perplexity over the arguments by
which they had been worsted, and which they knew
were altogether unfair even though they were unable
to point out the dishonest reasoning and the defective
links in the chain of evidence which had overcome
them when he challenged them to do so. With this
end now in view, Mitchell at once answered Mollie
with an air of alert and active interest, as though her
words had brought up a matter of vital importance.

"Wait a minute, my dear, I'm afraid I did not quite catch your meaning there. I understood you to say that unselfishness caused you to interfere when you heard me speaking unhandsomely of Warren behind his back. Now, what I fail to see is this : what has either selfishness or unselfishness to do with the matter any way?"

"Now, John Addison, you can't draw me into an argument this evening, so you might just as well give up the attempt now as later," Mollie answered, with a pretty impatience which made her even more charming than ever.

"I don't wish to draw you into any argument, Mollie ; but answer me, please. I am simply crushed under the burden of my own stupidity, and surely you will not be so cruel as to leave me in this miserable plight," Mitchell replied, in plaintive tones.

"I understand you perfectly, sir, and I have nothing to say."

"Oh, come now, Mollie, that's weak ; that's just a mere crawl," Mitchell scornfully exclaimed, trying to gain his point by provoking her through exasperation into the very discussion she was so evidently trying to avoid. Mollie saw through his scheme at once ; and she now showed the weakness with which he had charged her by permitting her annoyance to so far get the control of her feelings that she did answer his taunt, and so acted in exact compliance with his wishes.

"I will answer your question, but I want you to thoroughly understand that I will not get into any discussion with you," she replied, trying to convince

p

herself that she had not been badgered by him even into partial submission.

"That is all I have been asking for, my dear; a candid answer to an honest question is the only unfulfilled desire of my heart to-night. I have no more wish for a discussion than yourself," Mitchell returned, with brazen insincerity, inwardly chuckling over his success in managing his womankind, as he spoke.

"Very well, then," said Mollie. "What I meant was simply this: while I denied that I was a partisan in the present instance, I should still very much regret finding myself so constituted mentally and morally that I could never feel a profound, even an absorbing, interest in any person or any thing, except that person or object was associated in some way with my personal advantage."

"I see," Mitchell answered. "You mean that a person must possess a certain amount of unselfishness in order to make a good partisan."

"You agree with me, do you not?" she asked, replying to his implied question by directly proposing one herself. Then, as he returned no answer, she resumed her explanation of her idea, saying,—

"As I look at the subject, it seems to me that it is only the selfish, the cold-blooded, who never heartily 'take sides,' as the boys say, and who quietly weigh all the chances before they speak or act, in order to see just what and how much individual advantage they will gain by joining a cause or supporting a person. But I have answered your question, and in doing this I have done all that I promised to do; so good-night. Good-night, Effie." And with these words she retired to her tent.

Mitchell was not anxious to detain her, for the conversation, in more ways than one, had taken a turn he had not expected; while, in the insight it had given him into her mind, it had shown him feelings existing there he had by no means expected to learn that she entertained. All this required meditation, so he said nothing in reply to her last words, merely returning her "good-night;" and after she had disappeared within the tent he remained for some moments silently weighing all that she had said since the conversation first began, in all the bearings of her words. At last he said, thoughtfully, addressing his wife,—

"It seems to me, Effie, that I can see the outward and visible signs of a great inward change of feeling towards a certain young man of our acquaintance working in your sister; though perhaps the change has already been wrought in her."

"That is nothing new, dear; for you must remember that I prepared you for this shock some time ago."

"Well, hardly prepared me, for I did not more than half believe that you were right. But trust a woman for reading such signs correctly; you will detect them and note their meaning as soon, and even sooner, than our truthful friend yonder would discern an antelope's track," Mitchell answered, nodding towards Jim, who sat a little apart by himself placidly smoking his pipe.

"John," said his wife, laying her hand on his arm as she spoke,—"John, I beg of you, don't say or do anything absurd to influence her feelings."

Mitchell patted the slender fingers affectionately as he gave her the desired promise.

"I know what you mean, my dear," he said: "no

painful allusions to wardrobes are to be admitted; no reference to raiment is permissible. Be calm, my dear, be calm; no such words shall pass my lips. Even should we fall to discussing natural history, and should I find it necessary to speak of the elephant, even wild horses shall not drag from me the faintest or most distant allusion to his trunk."

Mrs. Mitchell laughed, and, rising to follow her sister into their tent, she answered,—

"I am very glad to hear you say so; but as we are none of us enthusiasts on the subject of natural history, and so long as we remain in camp we shall be out of the circus belt, I think a slight effort at self-control will be sufficient to keep you out of mischief."

Mitchell and his wife were altogether right in their suspicions. Mollie's feelings towards Warren, as her acquaintance with him advanced, and her knowledge of his character and of the man himself became more thorough, had undergone a complete change; though it would be more accurate to say that her sentiments had not so much changed as developed from a crude, undefinable condition, and had now passed into such a state that she herself could understand them and explain them.

From the first they two had been good friends. Notwithstanding the peculiar circumstances which had, for a time, opposed the formation of any friendship, and, by creating a feeling of embarrassed self-consciousness, at least on her side, had prevented a perfect understanding between them, she had always liked the man, and little by little she began to confess to herself that she did find a real pleasure in his companionship; while as for Warren, he was never so happy as when in her society.

Now, she had begun to understand her own mind, and to know that this liking was something more than a mere feeling of good-fellowship ; and she would have learned this truth long before she did awaken to it had not that pique to which her sister so often referred, arising from their first uncomfortable meeting, made her unwilling to give more than the merest courtesies of an acquaintance to one who had, however unintentionally on his own part, placed her in so disagreeable and ridiculous a situation.

Now, however, she felt within her heart a truth which she could not confess even to herself until its confession had been asked ; although she was obliged to admit that, should Warren try once again to win this confession from her, she would meet him differently from what she had done before. Then she found herself wondering would he ever try to win her again ? But this thought caused her very little anxiety, for she felt certain that he would ; and then she grew happy over the thought how, when the morrow had brought him, she would tell him how truly sorry she had been ever since she had heard of his terrible misfortune, and then—— But here she blushed, and refused to dream any further as yet, even in her own heart.

She had come now to recognize the truth that their natures were perfectly adapted, the one to the other ; he being strong, yet impulsive, while she was calm, yet fully as strong in her character, and at the same time gentle, sweet, and true.

Each gave to the other exactly those qualities which

that other needed; and the blending of their lives would be that uniting of sympathy to sympathy which makes two natures, each one in its support of the other, so wholly one that each recognizes its own imperfections when it exists apart from the other; while in the other each finds the most perfect happiness, the sweetest peace that earth can know; a blending of two natures which makes marriage a sacrament, a sacred mystery, prophetic of the perfect peace and happiness of heaven.

CHAPTER XV.

It was with a sore and heavy heart that Warren mounted his horse to rejoin his friend and resume his camp-life. The day was perfect in its every feature, perfect with all the beauty of a California morning. The air was sweet and filled with a balmy and refreshing warmth, while a soft, mellow haze clothed the distant mountain-peaks in a golden mantle.

Warren's mind was, however, occupied with thoughts which shut out all realization of the beauties which surrounded him. While the loss of his property was, of course, a serious blow, still, to so proud-spirited and ambitious a man as he the disappointment of his hopes was far more severely felt than the financial loss, heavy as it was.

He had confidently expected to see a large and prosperous town grow up on the Oakdale tract within the next two years,—or three at the outside,—which would ultimately develop into a thriving city. Not the least brilliant feature in this dream had been the hope of one day finding himself recorded in the annals of a great State as one of those far-seeing and public-spirited men whose almost prophetic prevision into the future of this fairest spot in all the nation had led them to give to the commonwealth the most beautiful of its garden cities.

But in the very hour when he was most fondly dreaming of success, in that same hour the spires and domes, the mansions and cottages of this fair city of

his visions vanished from before his eyes; and he woke
from his day-dream to see himself, like Alnaschar in
the Arabian tale, gazing upon nothing but the pitiful
relics of a shattered fortune.

The transformation in his own condition was no less
complete and no less mortifying than it had been in
the case of the visionary brother of the Oriental
barber, with whom he could not help contrasting
himself in his own mind. Instead of finding himself
foremost in the front rank of the leaders of nineteenth-
century development and American civilization, he was
so very far from becoming a great leader of progress, to
whom the founding of a city was no more of an achieve-
ment than the establishment of a successful business is
to ordinary men, that he found himself suddenly thrust
down from the high pedestal on which he had placed
himself to hold a place below the lowest of the hum-
drum and unenterprising men upon whom he had
hitherto looked down with pitying contempt; and
bitterest of all, in this humble estate he knew that
he was considered by others not a wreck of fallen
greatness, but only a broken speculator, a very commonplace and green young man, who had come from
the East to "astonish the natives," but had only succeeded in being relieved of the bulk of his fortune by
the first shrewd and plausible operator who wished to
take him in hand to pluck.

´ Being so much less than a hero in his own eyes, how
must he now appear, after all his boasting, in Mollie's
sight? And, of all the world, she was, to his mind,
the fairest and the sweetest, the one with whom he
most ardently longed to find favor.

When his prospects had been the brightest and his hopes the highest, he had never been able to win from her more than a cordial friendship. Now that he was nothing more nor less than a "boomer," even in his own estimation; now that the most partial of his friends would be compelled to speak of him as a speculator who had been beaten at his own game, and had come out of it a bankrupt and almost financially ruined, he could hope for nothing else from her than a pity almost worse for him to endure than her outspoken contempt.

He knew that he was going back to the camp almost for the single purpose of meeting her. He called himself a fool for his pains, and he told himself time and again as he rode along that if he were possessed of the smallest atom of sense he would turn back, write a note of excuse, and bid them all good-by, then pack up and be gone where he would never see her again, long before they could return. But all the while he was giving himself this excellent counsel he kept straight on in his course, and he knew that he could not follow out his own advice, however hard he were to try.

Warren had not yet learned that an ardent and devoted love such as that he gave to Mollie—a love which at once combined the poetry of passion with the sincerity of truth—could not fail to awaken the interest of the woman upon whom he lavished all the wealth of his affection. And though she might, for reasons of her own, withhold her love from him while his course was one of unclouded prosperity, yet when a great calamity overtook him her womanly nature would be so far from prompting her to manifest the cold sympathy of which Warren stood in fear, that his misfortunes would be the very thing wanting to induce her to give him the love he was striving to win, because she would know that this was *all* that she could do, while it would also be the best that she could do, to aid him in his conflict against trouble, and assist him in turning defeat into victory.

This was a truth that Warren had as yet to discover; and herein he was more fortunate than many men, for some men never have an opportunity of learning it, either because they are personally unworthy, or because they are unwise in their choice of the one upon whom they have bestowed their own affections.

A close concentration of our thoughts upon any one subject, whether the engrossing theme be pleasurable or painful, is a wonderful assistance to the flight of time, causing the minutes to roll on into hours, and the hours to fly by almost unperceived, and Warren now looked about him to find that his journey was almost two-thirds done. He had now come to the place where the road divided; the old road, long since abandoned for public use, and given over to chance passengers in the shape of tourists or hunters, here turned off to follow beside the channel of the twisting and winding creek, and skirting the spur of the mountain over which the new road, now invariably used, had been made. As he reached this point Warren reined in his horse, thinking for the last time that, as a sensible man, he ought to turn back and save himself from the humiliation that he knew awaited him if he followed his journey to its end; for the last time he made a strong effort to summon the resolution necessary to enable him to retrace his steps, but he could not. Either fate had some better thing in store for him, or else he had not yet suffered deeply enough to altogether satisfy the perverse fortunes ruling his destinies; so, with a sigh of pity for himself, and of compassion on his own weakness, he rode forward; though, to put off the hour which he felt could bring him nothing except evil, but yet which he had not sufficient force of character to altogether avoid, he turned off to take the old disused lower road as being the longer.

It was now almost noon; the mountains by which he was surrounded shut off the sea-breeze which, in places nearer the coast, cooled and tempered the air during the hottest days of summer. The fierce semi-tropical sun was beating down upon him from a cloudless sky with strong, burning rays. The haze had deepened on the mountains, as though nature, pitying their old and wrinkled features, had drawn a veil to soften their outlines in the eyes of human beholders. The intense stillness of this wilderness, at other times romantic, was now almost oppressive to Warren in his misery and loneliness. Not a sound broke the silence of the cañon except the occasional chirp of a cricket, the hum of a bee flitting from wild-flower to wild-flower, or the murmur of the brook at his feet. As he crossed the creek and rode out at the foot of the mountain to the place where the old road which he had been following met the new road as it descended the mountain spur, he was startled by the report of a gun far up the hill followed immediately by the cry of a woman, whose voice showed that she was either seriously hurt or else was in an agony of fear.

Warren stopped his horse to look up the steep grade, fearful lest some accident had occurred in this lonely spot; and, as if he were not yet miserable enough, to add to his wretchedness, he was about to become burdened with the responsibility of caring for a woman seriously wounded, and miles from any possibility of medical aid.

In a second, however, the current of his apprehensions became changed but not lessened, for a horse now came into sight plunging down the steep and narrow grade in all the blind frenzy of brute terror. His rider was a woman, and Warren's apprehensions became changed to the keenest anguish when he recognized the woman to be Mollie.

The road had been cut out of the side of the mountain, and while it was well kept and was in perfect repair, making it safe for a skilful driver, it was by no means the place in which a tyro ought to make experiments in feats of horsemanship, and it was a place of deadly peril in the event of a runaway. The road-bed was narrow, with the mountain wall on one side and on the other the sheer descent down, down hundreds of feet to the floor of the valley beneath. Should horse and rider plunge into that awful abyss they would both be dead before reaching the bottom, while Mollie would be torn and mangled beyond all possibility of recognition on the trees and bushes covering the mountain side like a *chevaux-de-frise* of nature's planting.

Warren saw the peril of the whole situation at the first glance, and, springing from his horse, he ordered him to stand, knowing that the well-trained brute would obey the command, however long his master might be absent; then he hastened up the steep road, intending either to rescue Mollie from her peril or to share her fate.

On he ran, at the same time being careful to avoid any sudden motion or any gesture of limbs or body that would add to the frenzy of her fear-maddened horse. So long as the animal kept to the smooth and carefully-tended road all was well; it was only a stumble, or some sudden apparition before him which might cause him to swerve to the right and plunge over the precipice, that Warren feared.

Since her first terrified scream Mollie had remained perfectly silent, and, so far as Warren could judge, she had recovered her calmness. She sat firmly in her saddle, holding her horse in with a strong, steady grasp, at the same time talking to him in gentle, soothing tones; but he had been too thoroughly maddened by fright to yield readily to his rider's influence, and he rushed wildly on down the steep descent. On, on he rushed, drawing rapidly nearer to Warren with every bound, and he in his turn ran with swift but cautious steps to meet the horse. As they came face to face, Warren stepped quickly to the very edge of the precipice, seized the horse by the bridle, and, throwing all his strength into his grasp, tried by a quick motion to back him against the mountain wall and hold him there until he could once more be brought under control.

One minute of quick resolution and awful action; one minute, seemingly endless in its duration. Above, the blue sky smiling in semi-tropical depth of color and richness of beauty; before them the mountain

wall, draped in vines of variegated foliage, and thickly
set with trees on whose branches the birds twittered as
they perked their heads and looked down in curious
wonder at the scene of human suffering and possible
death beneath; below, the yawning depths, through
which coursed the brook, smiling in the sunlight and
singing merrily as it hastened on to join its waters
with the ocean.

With the curious inconsequence which forms a part
of human nature in times of deadly peril, Warren
noted every detail of scenery and of event about him.
It seemed as though the very music of the creek came
up from the deep valley and reached his ears; while,
by a quick side-glance, as he seized the rein of Mollie's
horse when it dashed by him, he saw for the instant
his own horse quietly grazing by the roadside below,
careless of his master's fate.

Every trivial detail was borne in upon Warren's
mind for an instant; then, a strange humming filled
his ears almost deafening him; the very air seemed
filled with wild, staring eyes and open, frothing
mouths; earth and sky faded from before his sight;
the firm ground slipped from under his feet; he felt
himself hang in mid-air an instant; now he was falling down, down; once more a foot strikes, now rests
upon firm earth, now both feet stand secure, and all is
over.

How it was done, just what was done in those few
terrible seconds, neither Warren nor Mollie ever knew.
After one awful instant which seemed an eternity, and
during which he had passed through all the bitterness
of death, Warren found himself standing once more in

safety upon the mountain road, and firmly holding the horse, now subdued and trembling in every nerve, himself covered with sweat and dust, hatless, with torn clothes, bruised and bleeding. Seeing that the horse was once more quiet, he lifted Mollie, pale and, now that all danger was past, ready to faint, from her saddle; then, clasping her to his breast, he kissed her lips again and again, crying,—

"Oh, Mollie, my darling, my own sweet love, you are safe, you are safe! How thankful I am that I was brought here just in time!"

Mollie was so far from being outraged or even offended at this very unceremonious and unconventional treatment that she seemed to like it. She lay on his breast, clinging to him with a contented, happy, and restful feeling. It seemed to her, for the moment, that she belonged there, and while she remained there that she would be secure from every danger; so she held up her soft, sweet lips to his caresses, and returned them with the rapture which belongs to the first true love. For one moment of perfect happiness they gave themselves each to the other, and in that moment their souls were united for time and eternity; then Mollie remembered that this would never do on the high-road. What if the quail-hunter whose gun had caused the mischief should happen along? So she released herself from his embrace with a gentle motion, saying,—

"I am so glad and grateful, dear love, that *you* came to my rescue, and no one else.—But you are hurt?"

Warren looked down at his demoralized clothes and cut hands, as he laughingly answered,—

"I am bruised a little; personally I have met with

no more serious injury than that; as for my clothing, that is past repair, while my hat is gayly riding the waves of the creek on its way to the broad Pacific. You will have to ride back under the escort of one who, were an escutcheon given him, would be hailed as the Knight of the Deplorable Figure. Shall you be too much ashamed of my hatless and tattered plight to permit me to constitute myself as your guardian for the rest of the way?"

"Shall I, indeed?" Mollie answered, indignant at the bare thought. "I hope I am not quite a wretch. I think that you are the best and the bravest of men, and you never looked so lovely to me as you do at this moment. Every bruise and every hurt you have received in my service, and each one is a claim on my love. Come, now, let us go down to the brook and let me see how badly you have been hurt for me, you poor, brave, noble darling."

In vain Warren protested that he was not hurt in the least, and that he had never felt so well in his life as he did at that moment; Mollie would not be pacified until she had satisfied herself by a personal examination of his injuries; so together they walked down the road to the brook, Warren leading Mollie's horse and she walking by his side; and there, seated on a stone, she leaned over him washing the dust and blood from his hurts, while she kissed and petted him to his heart's content and praised him as the bravest of men, honestly believing—and what girl who had just been, like her, rescued from a great danger by her own lover would not have believed the same?—that he had performed a deed of unheard-of valor.

The day was the same in every way as it had been when Warren left Ventura, while it was only a few hours older, but the whole world had been changed for him in the events that had transpired in those few seconds on the mountain; such wonders can the briefest lapse of time work in all the rest of our existence. Then, Warren saw nothing before him but humiliation and a life-long struggle with a poverty of his own creation; now, although his fortunes had not mended in the least, the world looked bright, happy, and well worth the struggle it demands of every one who would live in it. The future seemed bright and promising now, and as for the poverty, it did not seem so very grinding or bitter after all, since Mollie had agreed to face it with him. Such a worker of miracles is a happy love.

Mollie soon found that her lover's words were true, and that, beyond a few bruises and slight cuts which needed no more careful medical treatment than court-plaster would supply, he had received no bodily injury at all. As she sat bathing these trifling hurts, she told him how she had happened to be at that place at all, and how the adventure had come about.

She began her story by mercilessly insisting upon one point, without paying the slightest attention to Warren's feelings, although she knew how fatal her words would be to the thoughts he was entertaining, and this was, that she had come out with no thought or intention of meeting him. She had been attracted by the beauty of the early morning, and by this alone, and having become, through her California residence, an accomplished horsewoman, as well as an enthusiastic lover of the exercise, she had gone out for the sake of the ride. It had proved pleasant, even beyond her expectations, and, charmed by the delicious air and exquisite scenery which no amount of familiarity can ever rob of its charms, she had prolonged her ride to the village of Nordhoff. Just as she had reached the top of the mountain on her return, a quail-hunter had startled her horse and herself by the unexpected discharge of his gun; "and," she added, with a pretty air of happy embarrassment, "you know the rest."

Warren made her an answer for the exact expression of which no language, so far as I know, has as yet added any adequate word to its vocabulary. Then, glancing up the mountain road, where a pedestrian figure could now be discerned in the distance coming down towards the spot where they were seated, he said,—

"Yes, and lest that man yonder should prove to be our quail-shooter coming to find out what mischief he has done, let us get on the road before he comes up to us to bore us with his excuses and apologies; and, perhaps, to suspect the happiness he has accidentally brought about."

Mollie blushed and gave a ready assent, and they were soon mounted and on the way once more.

The ride back was the happiest of the many they had taken in each other's company. The conversation was, however, nothing to which we would care to listen. Since the creation of man love-making has always been the same; it is an art whose principles and laws never vary, and the topics of conversation never change, while lovers themselves have never lost the happy faculty of making the people who are unfortunate enough to be brought into their company feel altogether uncomfortable and in the way. So we will spare ourselves the discomfort and our young friends the embarrassment of bearing them company on that ride, only saying in reference to it that, although courting on horseback does certainly possess marked disadvantages, on this occasion it held sufficient attractions to cause our young friends to strike a very moderate gait, taken, as I suspect, to prolong their ride to the utmost; although they deny this, and explain the length of time consumed in riding up the cañon to the badness of the road. However this may be, the fact remains that in making this trip theirs is the longest time on record, for it was late in the afternoon when they rode into camp, and were happy enough to find Mitchell and his wife alone, Jim being out catching trout for their breakfast.

Effie gave a little cry of alarm and dismay as she looked at Warren and saw the plight in which he had returned, while Mitchell made no attempt to conceal his astonishment at his friend's demoralized condition.

"Well, my deplorable friend, does the bursting of a boom in Southern California always shatter those within its range in this effective way?" he asked as soon as he recovered from his surprise sufficiently to be able to speak.

Warren assisted his companion to alight, then answered,—

"Like everything else in this wonderful country, a boom assumes colossal proportions; and consequently, when it goes off the splinters fly vigorously, filling the victims to such an extent that any one of them could pose as a model for Saint Sebastian, only that I know of none who have his look of calm resignation and quiet unconcern. In looking upon me, you see them all."

At this point Mollie interposed. ". John," she said, "you must not say one word about Mr. Warren's appearance, for he has been hurt in protecting me. My horse took fright when I was riding down the mountain, and right in its steepest part. Mr. Warren came by the old road, and just at the right moment. He saw it all, jumped off his own horse, ran to meet mine and stopped him at the risk of his own life. It was the bravest thing I ever knew. He saved my life and—and——" She stopped, partly because her voice was too full of the tears awakened by her conflicting emotions to permit any more lengthened explanation, partly because she did not know just what to say next. Warren took her hand, while Mitchell and his wife exchanged glances, grasping the whole situation at once.

"And you are going to give it to him as a reward for services rendered," he said, completing Mollie's sentence for her and glancing significantly at her hand as he spoke. "Well, a fair exchange,—you know the old saying, Warren. I congratulate you with all my heart; you have got a gem of a girl there, the best one in all the world, now that Effie has been submitted to cancellation. I am glad to welcome you as a brother; and I haven't wished you happiness, and am not going to, because there is no manner of doubt on that point. I've been in the family years enough to know what kind of women they are, and to speak with authority on that point. If you are not happy it will be all your own fault, my boy."

He shook his friend heartily by the hand, kissed his sister-in-law, and walked away, blowing his nose vigorously and grumbling something about so much strong sunlight being bad for catarrh.

Effie also went up to Warren to congratulate him, saying,—

"I have always liked you, Mr. Warren, and I am glad to know that Mollie is going to marry a brave man as well as a good one. I shall love you as I do my own brother; and saying that, I can say no more."

Warren thanked the pretty little woman, and at once availed himself of a brother's privilege, which she gracefully conceded, Mitchell looking on from one side and raising no objection.

They then seated themselves at the supper Effie had been preparing just as Jim arrived with a huge catch of trout. That experienced worthy, suspecting how matters stood, proceeded at once to extract the truth by a few skilfully-put questions.

"Wal," he remarked, "I didn't contract to take in no huntin' in this trip, 'n' I see 'tain't necessary. The jedge kin git 'long without me thar; 'n' he's done a right smart o' business at it, bringin' home the finest deer I've seen this season."

"Hold on, Jim," Warren answered, sternly. "No more of that if you ever want to see Ventura again. They often kill men out here for less than that."

"Oh, by the way, jedge," Jim went on, "that reminds me. 'Twuz jest two years ago to-day. I wuz out with a party over back o' Pine Mountain yonder——"

"Oh, shut up, Jim!" Mitchell exclaimed, breaking

21*

him off short in the beginning of his authentic anecdote. "We can't stand any more of your lies, or certainly not to-night."

Jim rose with an injured manner, saying, in a tone indicative of the profoundest grief at this unjust and inconsiderate treatment,—

"Lies! I want yer all to know, ladies 'n' gents both, that I hain't never yet said one word as wuzn't sollum gospel truth," and he went away to smoke his pipe in solemn meditation upon the possibilities of human ingratitude.

As he was now disposed of, for the evening at least, Mitchell turned to Warren and, assuming a manner of solemn importance, said,—

"Warren, as I am Mollie's nearest male relative,— I mean, of course, geographically speaking,—before I can bestow my final benediction upon your union I must inquire into your affairs closely enough to be sure that you can support a wife."

Warren laughed dubiously as he answered, "It is only fair that I should answer that question, or any other of a like nature that you may choose to put, owing to recent events; for these justify any doubts that may exist as to my financial soundness; while they are events which, whether they cast any shadows before them or not, certainly leave a heavy enough one behind."

Then he went on, speaking seriously and very sadly, to give a full description of his affairs as they were left by the failure of the Oakdale scheme, saying,—

"There is no use in my denying that you have been right and I have been wrong all along about this matter.

I have made an unmitigated ass of myself, and the pity of it is that it cost me almost all I am worth to find out how much of a donkey I am. I have crippled my means for many years, certainly, and I fear for life, for I have thrown away a little more than two-thirds of my fortune in my wonderful speculations. As for supporting Mollie as I could have done six months ago, that is now altogether out of the question. I cannot take her back to New York and keep up my home there; and, for the matter of that, I cannot live there myself as a bachelor in the old way any longer."

"I feared that you were hard hit. What do you propose, then?" Mitchell asked, looking very sober over this intelligence.

"I own a fine piece of ranch property here, just outside of the city limits. It is a good property, well stocked with fruit-trees and nuts, all in bearing condition. Fortunately for me, I bought it during one of my few lucid intervals, so I paid cash for it and do actually own it. I had thought that, if Mollie were willing, I would rent my house in New York and, after we are married, we would make this our home and live on the ranch, while I can practise my profession at the same time. From these different sources I could keep the wolf from the door of a very pretty home."

"You would continue to practise law in the new and approved method you have lately adopted, I suppose?" Mitchell asked, taking out a cigar and offering one to Warren as he spoke.

"Hardly," he replied, accepting the offer and taking out his match-safe. "I have had enough of booming in my six months' experience of it to last me through a very long life, should this be granted me. I am a child who has once been burned, and I am anxious to keep away from the fire for the rest of my life. With what I have saved from the wreck you can see that I would be wretchedly poor in New York; but out here we shall be rich, and we can enjoy all the luxuries that any reasonable mortal ought to ask for."

"Well, I don't see but what the picture is a pleasant one," Mitchell said, in a meditative tone, thoughtfully studying the ash on his cigar at the same time. "What do you think of it, Effie?" he asked, turning to his wife.

"I see nothing against Mr. Warren's plan," the sensible little woman at once replied, "while it seems to me that everything commends it. But, after all, it is not for us to decide in this matter; the question is one which Mollie must decide; she is the one whose life is interested. Can the recent city belle become transformed into a California matron and be happy in the change?" she asked, addressing her sister.

Mollie clasped her hands over her lover's arm, and glancing up into his face with eyes expressing the deepest love, she answered,—

"I am willing to do whatever is right and for the best, and I know that I shall be happy. Then, after all, I prefer fruits and flowers to ice and snow; and you know how happy I have been in the free life we have been living all these months, and ask no better fate than to continue it. I have eaten the lotus and I have forgotten my old home. Yes, I can say that I am glad that it is best for us to live here."

"That settles it," Mitchell answered, emphatically. "And as you say, Warren, although you would be a poor man in the East, you will be a rich one out here; while, by doing as you propose, and by sticking closely to legitimate business, you will stand a good chance to recuperate your fortunes. But let me give you one word of caution that may help you in your domestic management: I think it would be by far the better plan for you to leave the buying of your wife's wardrobe wholly in her hands. But if you should ever feel inclined to exercise your own taste in selecting her apparel, I beg of you, for goodness' sake, don't provide for her as you did once upon a time."

Mollie blushed and looked unutterably wretched.

"John!" his wife exclaimed, looking sternly upon him; and the one word emphasized by her glance conveyed volumes of meaning.

Warren rose and stood over him threateningly.

"Mitchell," he said, "if ever you mention that circumstance again, I shall inflict upon you grievous bodily injuries; and I promise you that they shall be severe, for I shall cover your whole person with bruises."

"I am crushed again. Personal attire no longer has any place in my knowledge, and even the very names by which the articles are designated are, from henceforth, expunged from my vocabulary. I will promise to go to bed at once, also, if you'll forgive me."

"We will be most happy to excuse you, John, and I think you had better go," Mollie replied, severely.

Left to themselves the lovers sat until late in the night telling one another those incidents which are drawn from the inexhaustible fund of themes always at the command of two people in love.   As they parted for the night Mollie shyly whispered,—

" I am afraid, dear, that I have given you something you do not much care for and did not want, after all."

" What is that?" Warren asked, greatly surprised.

"Myself," she answered, looking down upon the ground, and prettier than ever in the clear light of the full moon.   " Do you know, you have never once asked for me, or even said that you wanted me to be your wife?   It would be dreadful if I had been mistaken all along; and how am I to know that I have not?"

You know full well the answer that he made her.

THE END.

Printed by J. B. Lippincott Company,
Philadelphia.